The Remedy

P.J.LAW

Published in 2008 by YouWriteOn.com

Copyright © P.J.Law 2009

First Edition

The author asserts the moral right under the Copyright, Designs and Patents Act 1988 to be identified as the author of this work.

All Rights reserved. No part of this publication may be reproduced, stored in a retrival system, or transmitted, in any form or by any means without the prior written consent of the author, nor be otherwise circulated in any form of binding or cover other than that in which it is published and without a similar condition being imposed on the subsequent purchaser.

Published by YouWriteOn.com

For my family

Acknowledgements

The following people have been great sources of support, advice, encouragement and love in the writing of this novel and I would like to thank them very much: Brendan Armstrong, Colin Cooper, Shirley Coulson, Gillian Nineham, Seamus Waldron, Kerri Wilkinson, the staff of the Wychwood Brewery and most especially, my mum and dad, Yvonne and Roy.

ONE

Dorothy Ford died in circumstances that were never clear or explained fully to her youngest daughter, Erica. For a fifteen year-old girl, it was a tragedy so shocking and untimely that she was made mute in her grief for several months, propelled to the bosom of her older sisters and to her father, who fought between them to fill her void. Ten years on and the desolation of it all pricked at her still, her rudimentary grope through adulthood constrained by a simmering dissatisfaction.

Now, when Erica was brought up short by events in the news or by the exposure of blemishes in the fabric of her family, the past came back to her like a malignant storm, thrashing through her consciousness. She was frightened that someone or something would come and find her, hurt her, take the stability of her life with her father and break it up irreconcilably as it had done before.

And she had good reason.

It was seven o'clock in the morning. Erica was eating toast, standing at her post by the radio, her eyes flicking over the jagged contours of the cluttered kitchen. The headlines of the day's news crackled into the room from a shabby metal radio and Erica peered out of the window as she listened. A thick drizzle hung in the air and it was difficult to make out even the heftier trees that lined the perimeter of the garden. The daffodil heads were heavy with moisture and the lawn was a shadowless grey green. Erica thought back to the seventies and to her mother planting spring bulbs. A quiver caught her chin. She looked back into the room, to photographs stuck to the refrigerator and took a last swig of tea from her mug.

Yesterday morning another woman was assaulted in the Brenly-on-Thames area.

Erica held the warm liquid in her mouth, unable to swallow for a moment.

The woman, a nurse in her forties, was returning home from work at 6.30 a.m. when she was attacked by a man on her doorstep. The police believe he was trying to break in to the woman's house but ran from the scene when disturbed by her husband. He is described as white, six foot tall, with grey-brown hair. Police are appealing for anyone who has information as they believe he could strike again.

Erica swallowed, gasping briefly for breath.

Brenly was where she lived, in a shabby old stone rectory. Brenly was a place that was somewhere between village and small town, where there was little to report bar the digging of the roads and Saturday night joy riders from the city's estates.

Her thoughts were disturbed by the sound of her father moving about upstairs. She switched the radio off and opened the back door to a fine spray of freezing mist. Bending to reach the nearest clump of daffodils the air picked up and a light wind pushed a few strands of hair over her face. A movement beyond the trees caught her eye and she looked up, her anxieties waiting to pounce; they tickled her paranoia, chuckling at the trick of the light and Erica fought to dismiss them.

She snapped urgently at a dozen stems and walked hastily back towards the house willing herself not to turn around. Once in, Erica bolted the door and leant against it, panting, a swell of heat rising up her back.

"Christ." She said. "This is nuts."

She laid out breakfast things for her father on the long oak table, placing the flowers in a vase in front of them. Hastily collecting her bag from the hallway, she called up the stairs.

"Bye dad."

"Bye love." Came a muffled response from the bathroom.

Pausing at the entrance to the dining room, Erica took in the vision of the three shotguns that hung above the fireplace for what felt like the first time since her childhood. The room was a stale, lifeless annexe that no one had entertained in since she was a child, but today the dusty guns, their barrels black and greasy from a former life, held her gaze.

A toilet flushed upstairs and Erica started. She lunged at the front door with a clammy hand and slammed it shut behind her to stroll bravely across the gravel. Shunting her car into gear she set off for work, manoeuvring inexactly, kicking up gravel in her wake.

Harry Ford leant into the deep windowsill from the first floor landing and watched his daughter skit about the driveway, a feeble smile on his lips, his hand pressed against the glass in frozen salutation.

Though the morning passed quickly at work, Erica was relieved when her boss disappeared to a working lunch and left her alone. She turned to read her private messages that had come through that morning. Erica flicked through them and replied briefly. There were three from her sisters inviting her to various functions, which amused her to note their attempts to obliquely reference one another. Between the two of them, they had claimed a piece of her for the remaining weekends in March, adding a casual 'PS' to ask if they could pick her up on Saturday to drive to the cemetery.

Erica stopped twiddling a lock of hair around her index finger and sat back from her desk. She knew they would be visiting the grave, but not all four of them together. It would be too weird.

She yanked at a hair band that was holding back a wedge of brown springy locks from her eyes and snapped it onto her wrist. Pulling on her thick wool coat she strode out of her office, head down, hair as a shroud over her reddening face taking in the landscape of the university offices where she worked. The contours of the older buildings stood graceful and shadowless in the breaking haze, softening the impact of the boxy sharp-edged modern blocks that housed most of the science faculty.

Erica walked slowly, following the wall of the building with her hand, rebelling against the cold with an unbuttoned coat, a chill agitating her neck and the small of her back. Taking an entire lap of the building, she passed small groups of students twittering in huddles and enjoyed her apparent invisibility to them made more evident she supposed, since she graduating from student to member of staff. Leaning back against the cold brick she breathed deeply, shivering, searching for stamina against the elements, eyeing people scuttling around in soft focus, their forms muted in the misty air.

By the weekend, the temperature had dropped to freezing and the threat of snow hung like a weighty shroud over the morning. Erica and Harry had taken breakfast in separate rooms and the sound of the gravel churning in the drive brought them both to the front door.

Erica's sisters sat in a hefty four-wheel drive with the engine and the stereo on, doors closed. She leapt out to greet them, a coat thrown over one arm, hair tied back carelessly into loose band.

"Morning!" Erica chirped as she got in to the car. They exchanged kisses, commented on the weather and settled into a lively banter. Harry came out a few minutes later clutching an old sack that rustled and clanked as he walked.

"Hi girls." He said.

They waved distractedly at their father from their seats.

He knocked on the window. "I've got some autumn bulbs to plant and a few other bits and pieces. I'll put them in the boot shall I?" He looked meaningfully at his eldest daughter, Janice, who got out to open the boot for him, returning hastily to the driver's seat. Erica strained to hear if they spoke but the noise of the radio and the conversation meant she caught nothing.

As they drove away from Brenly heading west through a tumble of low hills, snow began falling in fine lacy sheets. The time spent in the car was a chance for them all to catch up on each other's news without mentioning the purpose of the journey itself. Half an hour on and the curtains of snow had thickened and were billowing over the car, their obeisance to aerodynamics leaving the windscreen untouched by a single flake. The occupants stared with fixed concentration at the road ahead despite Janice's careful manoeuvring.

"It's left here," said Harry leaning forward to direct from the back seat.

"Yes dad, we know."

"We should come here on mum's birthday too you know." Said Harry. "We might have better weather."

"We *do* come on mum's birthday dad." Said Ellen politely, the middle of three siblings.

Harry shuffled in his seat, searching for a new tangent and found one in the form of asking his daughters if they would all be coming to his company's annual ball. They said that they would and the girls moved easily into talk about parties and friends, theatre and gigs, this and that.

"I'll be inviting Francoise again I expect." Said Ellen boldly. "To the ball."

Erica nodded. "I'll need to sort Duncan out if I'm to bring him I think. I mean, he came into my office this week wearing odd socks and with sticky tape on the arm of his glasses. He's a total geek."

Janice giggled. "Take him shopping. Sort him out."

A half smile formed on Harry's wide mouth and his grey eyes were unfocused. He leant his head against the window and let the banter of his daughters wash over him. By the time they reached the cemetery he felt sleepy and so removed from the conversation that Erica had to prompt him to make a move.

The church was quiet and the fields around it deserted.

Aside a couple of impenetrable yews that flanked the cemetery gates, it was a bare landscape of crooked headstones tipped with snow, laid out in neat rows around an isolated Cotswold church. They walked in silent file around the nave, pressing light prints into the path.

Erica's pace quickened as they reached the spot.

"God the flowers are all bent!" She crouched down to brush the snow off a neat line of daffodils that edged their mother's plot. Harry laid his sack on the ground and put his hand on her shoulder.

"S'alright love, there'll be more next year. They won't have died." He said with a reassuring pat.

Erica, tormented by the sight of snapped narcissi, systematically and unsuccessfully pulled the flowers upright. "Jesus you bloody things, stand up!"

Reaching from an unstable squat, she moved onto her knees, scrabbling for twigs and woody detritus to prop up the flowers that were buckling from a weight of snow.

Janice and Ellen passed a concerned exchange and synchronously bent down to join their sister in her task.

Harry watched, his hands in his pockets, and after a minute, pulled out a large white handkerchief and passed it down to Erica. She accepted it wordlessly, passing it back when she had finished without looking up.

The grave had become a mess of disturbed snowfall and earth amid an otherwise pristine landscape. Harry knew better than to suggest they churn up the ground further by digging in autumn bulbs when the girls had finished. They stood opposite him looking down at their handiwork: Erica, in the centre, tall and uncomfortable in an ill-fitting duffle coat, flanked by her sisters, shorter, wider and more sturdy in jeans and heavy trainers. All silent, heads cocked, melting silent flakes of snow in their hair.

Harry looked at them, taking them in, his progeny that barely resembled each other and who, aside Erica, owed him little for what they had made of their lives and who they had become. Erica at least was her father's daughter in looks – lanky, shamelessly inelegant but striking for her leanness and height and the thick curls that covered her head.

He glimpsed at Janice, her mother's physical replica, his eyes flicking back urgently to Erica and back to Janice again.

She looked up and caught Harry's gaze. He returned the hard penetrating stare that met him with a weak smile that quickly crumbled, the edges of his mouth sliding back into a thin, flat line. Janice, unblinking, and discernable only to Harry, shook her head slowly from side to side in tiny movements.

The moment was broken by Erica who was brought back to the reality of standing hatless in a snow shower in a cemetery. "I meant to bring a flask." She offered, a heavy shiver briefly knocking her off balance. "But I forgot. I have done in the past."

"Hardly the weather for a picnic." Said Harry, glad of the return to safer conversation.

"Maybe the ground's too hard dad." said Erica nodding to his sack. "And anyway, if we planted autumn bulbs now, we might disturb the lupins and delphiniums and all the other stuff. That's the problem with perennials. They vanish to nothing in the winter."

"Only you could try and recreate an entire cottage garden in a space that's six foot by four foot." Said Ellen squeezing Erica's shoulder. "I came by last June, I remember. Surrounded by all these dismal headstones and then there's one with all these purple and red flowers and I thought 'that'll be Erica then'."

Erica smiled. "I do my best."

"A fitting tribute love. We all know how much mum loved the garden." Said Harry.

"We all know how much mum loved *life*." Janice's tone split the air between them and Harry's smile was shot down again. He shrank back, retreating into his thick winter coat.

Erica, head cocked and eyes unfocussed on her mother's headstone, seemed oblivious. There was silence again between them, punctuated only by the intermittent bark of crows and the family's own disjointed contributions. Janice idly stoked Erica's coat sleeve – playing the reassuring elder sibling – and turned back through the cemetery slowly and respectfully, retracing her tracks through the loosely compacted snow.

"Right, well, d'you know, we've come all this way but it is freezing and I'm wondering if we should just head back." Said Ellen returning to the moment, brightly, falsely.

Erica frowned, aware suddenly of Janice's departure. She looked at Ellen for an explanation.

Harry collected his sack from the ground moving gingerly as if to muffle the solemn clank of rusty garden forks. "You're right love. It *is* freezing. We picked the wrong day…"

His voice was shallow and low and it pricked Erica to see the undulations of his mood. She held her frown throughout the slow procession back to the car and opened her mouth to speak, closing it again, firing a few questioning looks to Ellen in the hope of some response. Ellen shrugged her shoulders and started on a lengthy diatribe about the football season.

Ford family equilibrium restored – everyone to their own agenda, all parties' thoughts hidden by an irregular, stilted babble.

During the drive back the snow fell in a dusty continuum and the four eventually sat quietly listening to the radio. On entering Brenly, they were diverted to an alternative route to the house. Police had cordoned off the street and Janice pulled over to enquire of an officer the reason why.

He bent down to speak into the window. "There's been another incident similar to the one last week. Happened early this morning but we were only alerted a few hours ago. All residents will be contacted in due course. Do you live in this road?"

"No. But my sister does." Janice said waving her hand towards the back seat.

"Fine. You can make your way through."

The police officer peered briefly into the back of the car. A man in his late fifties peered back, a straight wide line for a mouth, a mop of curly grey hair in disarray over his forehead. Next to him, the terrified blue eyes of a young woman looked through him. Her mouth was open as if frozen in the act of forming the letter *W*, her hair a mirror of her father's in its contours but its shock of black made more prominent by the pallor of her skin.

As they pulled away he glanced sideways through the window again and met Erica's eyes a second time.

TWO

Duncan's disappointment at his girlfriend's apparent lack of interest in seeing him for a few days was short lived. The week passed without event and he was content to muddle along with his own amusements. It stretched his patience though when she declared that she was also unavailable at the weekend due to a family outing.

"But you don't do things as a family." He had protested. "And you've been over at the brewery every night after work."

He sat staring at the screen of his computer, the central hub of his bedroom. It was placed amid boxes of electronic equipment and games, Duncan's clothes and shoes strewn in a wide arc. In one corner of the room was a small chest with framed photographs of his family, both alive and ancestral, some spilled packets of incense and a couple of dusty candles. There was no television, no curtains and only a single lamp to light the room.

Duncan was content in his world, retaining the chaos that surrounded him with a rebellious pride. He did not lead a penurious existence, evident from the outlay he lavished upon his more technically oriented hobbies, and although he complained at Erica's lack of visits to the flat, he was not sufficiently motivated to tidy it up.

He clicked and tapped at his computer, typing, deleting, retyping and pushing the Enter key with satisfying smacks. Duncan was four hours into an online role-playing game and had been sitting in the same position for the duration. His knee bounced up and down at speed largely because he was well overdue a visit to the toilet and when he wasn't rolling the mouse for his next move, he idly bit the skin around his nails.

The phone rang and he jumped.

"Damn!"

He raced around with the mouse control to save his position and fumbled to find his phone. Seconds after it had rung out he dialled to collect the message that had been left.

Hi, it's me. I'm assuming you're up to your neck fighting monsters on the Planet Ping, because let's face it, you're hardly likely to be leafing through racks of John Rocha in Debenhams of a Saturday afternoon. Pause. *Give me a ring. I'm at home.*

"John Rocha?" Duncan asked out loud and dialled Erica's number. "Hi, it's me. I couldn't find the phone."

"Quelle surprise. What are you up to? No, don't tell me. Please. You're at it again." Erica said wearily.

"Err, well, yes. But I've almost finished and I only started at eleven today."

"Duncan, it's after three."

"What? No way. I thought it was about twelve."

Erica exuded a weighty sigh.

"I thought you were busy today – oh god, sorry, I mean, how did it go?"

Erica spoke quietly. "It was weird. The journey was weird, the conversation was weird and well, basically, my whole family are weird."

"Ah. How long did you stay there?"

"Not long, not in this weather. I don't really know why we went."

Duncan looked out of the window and saw the snow for the first time that day. "Bloody hell it's snowing! Fantastic. Let's meet up somewhere, if you're free now that is, which I'm assuming you are, which is why you called."

"Jesus Duncan. It's been snowing all mor—"

"Wow. It's settling too. In March! Bring it on."

"Duncan, there's been another attack in Brenly. Our street was cordoned off when we got home. Apparently it started off as a burglary again but the bloke got interrupted or something. So I don't particularly feel like coming out to meet you and leaving dad here on his own. Not today, of all days. But you're welcome to come over if you like."

"Oh god, that's awful. Is it connected to the one last week? Have you spoken to the police? Have your sisters gone?"

"I haven't spoken to the police but dad was just talking to our neighbour and he said it might all be connected. And yes, Janice and Ellen have gone. They didn't even come in. Typical."

"Oh, OK." Said Duncan. "Hmm. Ah. Well I'll come over in a bit."

"OK, good. I'll cook. See you later."

"Oh Erica, one more thing. Who's John R—?"

The phone clicked and Erica was gone.

Duncan hastily Googled John Rocha and on discovering that he was a clothing designer, was nonplussed. He surveyed his collection of cotton t-shirts and chinos that were heaped around the room, scooped them up and threw them into the wardrobe. He padded off to his flat mate's room, plucked the most rigid-looking shirt from his cupboard and slid a folded jumper from a pile of fresh laundry.

He arrived at Erica's house within an hour of their conversation. Duncan waived politely to Harry who was fiddling about in the greenhouse despite the fading light and made his way to the kitchen.

Erica was busy over the hob, face flushed and sleeves rolled up to the elbows. "I see you're wearing Andy's clothes again." She commented dryly, making an obvious gesture of looking him up and down.

Duncan, opened his mouth to speak but closed it again, frowning.

"Not that I mind." Erica added, smiling now. "You obviously got the shopping reference then."

"Yes, thanks for that."

"Well, as long as Andy doesn't mind."

Duncan said nothing for a moment and set about arranging stray breadcrumbs into a line on the table. "I don't like shopping Erica, and I definitely don't have time for it. And we've had this conversation before."

"Duncan, you spend half your life on the Internet. Go shopping there." Erica said carelessly.

"Yes, but I might have to send things back and that's just too much aggro. Besides, you are my designated follower of fashion. Get me some stuff and I'll pay you."

"No way. We'll go shopping in town together sometime."

"Erica, why the renewed interest in my clothes? Granted I wear a lot of industry t-shirts, and granted I get them free, but in my line of work it doesn't really matter what you wear."

"Andy works in IT. *He* has decent clothes."

"But Andy's English and English blokes are always poncing about with their clothes."

Erica paused from her station to take in Duncan's stooped form at the table. "English blokes are not always *poncing* about with their clothes and while we're on the subject, I saw some pretty well-dressed blokes in Edinburgh last summer I'll have you know."

"They were probably English. And anyway, you're not exactly the Stella McCartney of Brenly are you?" Grinning now, he held up his hands to shield his face.

Erica's mouth twitched in and out of a smile and she set back to the hob, stirring a pan with an oversized spoon. "I am sort of like Stella." She mused. "We both lost our mothers during adolescence."

By reference to her mother, the humour of the moment was instantly extinguished and Duncan sank back into his chair.

"Yes but was your mum's legacy a multi-million pound vegetarian sausage-making empire?" Duncan scowled into the middle distance, his knee bouncing up and down. And is Stella McCartney acting like her mum just passed away yesterday?

It was Erica's cue to bring him back round. "Dad's got the May ball coming up at work, so you might like to get something new for that." She said in a brighter tone.

"Is that your way of asking me to come with you?"

"Yeah..."

"Well I'll check my diary and get back to you. I might have something on."

Erica had her head down, concentrating on two pans, tasting her fare and seasoning as she went, but between thick locks of hair that hung over her face, she poked her tongue out.

Duncan, smiling easily now, launched into describing the alluring financial possibilities presented by writing databases for small businesses on the side. He explained how keen he was run the idea past her having received only luke warm encouragement from Andy. Erica nodded agreeably giving half an ear to Duncan's plan and looking pensively out of the window at Harry, still fiddling obsessively by half-light in the greenhouse.

The Ford family had gone their separate ways on returning from the cemetery. Erica had slumped onto the sofa, flicking through TV channels with a brief respite to call Duncan, and Harry had retreated to the garden. After half an hour of chewing at her frayed nails and flicking through a magazine, she had wordlessly taken a cup of tea out to her father and returned to prepare a meal in the kitchen.

Duncan's voice was noise in her head that came in and out of focus alongside her own thoughts. She wanted to go out, to drink, dance, fall over, or put herself in the path of possibility, but there would be no such temptation this evening. She wanted something to happen, beyond her own narrow influences: a good thing, an anything, a counter thing. Although time spent with Duncan was notoriously academic or themed in a geeky, repressive manner, he could be the lubrication between her and Harry, allowing them to move around each other in the chilly spring evening. It was easy to set up and it was stimulation free.

The doorbell rang and she jumped.

"It's OK, I'll go." She said.

Erica found Harry talking to a police officer in the driveway and recognised him as having been the same man that Janice had stopped in the street earlier in the day.

She fumbled with her hair, offered a quiet *Hello* in response to the man's greeting and looked down at her feet as he introduced himself. She hovered by the door as he offered her a crudely printed leaflet of neighbourhood awareness facts. Her observations of him were simple and immediate: he had a deep voice, a solid wide frame and as he handed her the leaflet, she noticed long fingers and well-manicured nails.

"There's going to be a short presentation by the team investigating these incidents at the Five Bells pretty soon. We're urging as many people to come as possible, especially if you're at all concerned for your safety. Hopefully we'll have it all wrapped up by then, but you never know."

They stood, holding either end of the crudely printed sheet for the moments that it took for him to explain these facts.

"Right. Thanks." Said Erica. "I'll be there."

"Good." Said the police officer, the skin creasing endearingly around his eyes as he smiled. He let go and Erica felt herself blush, caught up in her own bashful response. She heard the scrape of a chair from the kitchen, and turned quickly to go back in to the house, keen to thwart any attempt made by Duncan to join her on the doorstep.

Janice stood in front of the large Belfast sink and moved her hands under soapy water to find the last piece of cutlery. Ellen sat eyeing her sister from behind, cupping a mug in her hands, feet up on a long pine bench. The light of the day was diminishing by degrees behind a thick grey sky, and the reflection of the snow outside cast a bluish border to the window frames. Janice hastily wiped around the sink and turned to see Ellen observing her. She dried her hands on her apron and fiddled with a clip to pull her hair loose. It sat in a sensible grey and blond bob on her shoulders and seemed to Ellen to cap the image of a thirty-four-year old going on fifty.

"What?" Asked Janice frowning.

"Nothing." Said Ellen and reached into a tall tin marked *Biscuits*. She wore a collection of heavy silver rings that clanked as she rummaged about.

"You won't find any chocolate ones. Cleo will have polished them off." Janice commented, opening the fridge and peering in for something.

"Want one?"

"No thanks. What are these?" Janice asked patting her hefty backside.

"Yes, but you're like mum's family. So no amount of abstinence is ever going to change the way you look."

"Cheers."

"And you have a family who all love you so don't give me the *a-tti-tude* and take a bloody biscuit."

Janice abandoned the fridge and joined her sister at the table.

"I meant to say, I like your hair like that. Red suits you."

"Thanks." Said Ellen. "It was Francoise's idea. I think it's a bit bright though. Seems to clash with everything apart from black."

They ate noisily and listened to the sound of heavy movement from above and children's voices. Ellen had made herself comfortable in the kitchen on return from the cemetery, huddled up on a bench next to the old stove. She pondered how she might broach the subject of Janice's behaviour during the day, and in doing so, had created long silences between them.

"Cleo's ever so good to be looking after the boys today." She said.

"She is. She's also grounded. Keith caught her with hash last weekend." Janice reached out for another biscuit. "As in marijuana."

"Ah well, I guess that's what they all do these days." Ellen paused. "I certainly did."

"Well she's not a kid anymore so she should know better. I know, I know." Janice held up her hand. "He's ever so strict on them though – Keith – I try and make it up to Cleo in other ways."

"*He's* strict on them?" Ellen ventured.

The sound of boys' voices from upstairs grew and Janice looked up at the ceiling. "I should have left them outside."

Ellen nodded, leaning back into the wall and asked quietly. "So are you going to call Erica later?"

Janice silently picked at a knot in the long pine table.

"I did wonder what today was all about and I'm sure Erica will be too." Ellen paused. "I'm not having a go Janice. I just thought we were meant to be moving on." She bit her lip and waited.

"How can we possibly move on for as long as that monster is still on the planet?" Janice spat, biscuit crumbs spraying the table.

"OK OK, calm down. I just thought, you know, well, I'm just not sure why you wanted me to organise a trip for the four of us. We only stayed there ten minutes." She hesitated. "And please don't call our dad a monster."

Janice glared back at her sister for a second. There was a hefty thump from above and in three nimble strides she was at the door.

"Will you keep that racket down!"

The thumping stopped and after a few moments a girl's voice came back. "Sorry!"

Janice hovered in the doorway for a second before slowly padding back to the table.

"OK, I'll call her later. Or tomorrow. I thought it would be a good idea, the whole cemetery thing. I just forget how much he irritates me. I'll say it was hormones, or I'll blame the kids for a sleepless night or something."

Ellen drew her knees in, tilting towards the stove for warmth. "Don't play the hormone card. Erica gets it worse than us. Say it was sleep. But you need to say something."

Janice reached for the biscuit tin for a third time and Ellen pulled it out of her reach looking through layers of thick mascara and cocking her mouth in a half smile.

"OK." Said Janice, defeated. "But you know that Erica's been making noises about moving home, feeling unsettled and stuff."

"And?"

"And, well, she's twenty-five now and maybe it's time to explain a few things. It might be a catalyst to get her out of the old house."

Ellen pulled an open mouth but Janice continued. "Well maybe not the whole story. Maybe just bits of it."

"Which bits did you have in mind exactly? I'm not shattering that girl's life by digging up the past. And don't you dare think of doing it either. She's wedded to that house. And to dad."

"God I know. I know. I was praying she'd end up at uni in Exeter or Glasgow or somewhere. She's brainier than me but she's got no ambition." Janice leant forwards to hook the rim of biscuit tin with her nail and draw it towards her. "Brainier than both of us put together." She added.

"You're a bloody doctor." Said Ellen emphatically.

"Was." Her jaws moved hastily and she swallowed. "Means nothing. How many times did I resit?" She asked miserably.

"Well anyway. We need to think this one through. You can't act normally in front of dad and you won't explain to Erica what your problem is with him so sooner or later she's going to ask, or worse, she'll hear something and it'll come out another way. What would you prefer?"

The kitchen clock clicked out the seconds, and then minutes, between them. A lamp a on a timer flicked on in the hall and Janice idly looked over to the corner of the room, eyelids heavy.

She sighed and spoke quietly. "I'll ring Erica. But I'm not telling her anything. And I'll go to that stupid ball and I'll behave myself. That OK?"

"That's OK. Thanks." Said Ellen. She shuffled forward and kissed her sister lightly on the cheek. "I manage to pull it off alright. You should too. I'd much rather we lived a life of pretence just now to protect our little sis than start rattling the ghosts in the closet. And anyway, it's up to dad to tell her everything." She stood up and stretched. "I'm gonna head. I need to be back in London by seven."

Ellen gathered up her things and called up the stairs to say goodbye to the children.

Janice, still picking at the knots in the table turned to her. "Is that Singh woman still Erica's boss?"

THREE

It was another fortnight before Erica heard any more about the incidents in Brenly. Had the snow come in December it would have charged the spirits of everyone over Christmas, but in spring it brought anxious journeys for commuters and irritation for farmers. As the temperature lifted and white flakes gave way to heavy rain, banks of waving yellow diminished to drooping brown heads as the brilliance of the early spring beds receded for another year.

It drew Erica out into the garden in the lighter April evenings to swiftly dead-head and rake up the detritus of winter. It was an act that signified to her father that the mourning period was over which brought them both into conversations about plans for vegetables and fruit that would be grown that year.

In the garden of the Old Rectory, the ferns emerged in tight coils, hugging the shady patches around the perimeter wall and in the more wooded parts. Erica took time to crouch by them and pull gently at the loaded springs. Though she did this every year, it was with the delicate anticipation of a child testing the physics of nature for the first time. New horse chestnut leaves hung like limp hands before opening out, their branches playing host to a renewed skittering and a change in the birdsong that pulled Erica's gaze upwards. The tulips, fresh and rarer beasts than the swathes of narcissus, cut a shock of red and pink in well-planned clumps, the fattest heads destroyed in a day by a single downpour. Commuters that were dreamers spent their journeys home gazing west into the early evening sunset. Erica among them, saw banks of clouds behind lines of trees become the silhouette of mountain ranges, their forested foothills in the foreground.

A further leaflet drop in the village re-immersed Erica into the charged anxiety of the damp morning that she had heard of the first burglary, and her joy for spring temporarily receded. She cleared her diary for the evening that the police would be meeting with the villagers and resigned to go alone whether Harry was free or not. She pondered on the emphasis of the thing – would it be a blow-by-blow verbal and visual reconstruction of the burglaries in an attempt to jog people's memories, or a lecture on the merits of neighbourhood awareness? Either way, Erica's resolve to attend lay in the borderline of her subconscious; she would attend because she ought to show her face – the straightforward, socially uncomplicated face of Erica Ford that lived in the Old Rectory – and because there was the possibility that the same police officer would also be there.

The incidents had troubled Erica in a way that was beyond the boundaries of any relationship in her life to explain. Her sleep was disturbed by tortuous anxieties and her concentration at work began to suffer. Her boss seemed to be paying keener attention to her work and to her movements, and despite the awareness of her own conscientious reputation, Erica felt she was under scrutiny. Coupled with an unshakeable tiredness, she had taken to visiting one of the university's more distant campus libraries in the mornings, feigning meetings with colleagues.

The librarians were, in Erica's opinion, stern-faced women who added a distinctly menopausal edge to their interactions with staff and students and Erica made a point of moving past them to quieter recesses. For her, the library had an instantly calming effect. She became heavy and slow-moving to the point of wanting to lie down and sleep on the comfortless nylon carpet. On finding the right spot, she joined in with the students who did practically that: a hand propping up a chin gave way to a head on a desk and a futile attempt to read text side-on, which inevitably gave way to sleep. As long as no one was actually snoring, these essential acts of intellectual rejuvenation went largely ignored by the library's militia.

However, Erica was struggling to keep her naps to a respectable length of time and caught a suspiciously raised eyebrow from her boss one morning on returning to the office.

"Erica, I'm going to be out all afternoon but I've just emailed you some things that I'd be grateful if you could follow up."

"No problem."

"If you have time of course."

"Yes I do."

Her boss, Professor Anita Singh, smiled in a way that said unequivocally in Erica's view: *The militia informed me that you've been seen napping in the library.*
Erica blushed and added. "It's fine."

"Good. Any problems, call me on my mobile. I'll see you tomorrow."

Professor Singh grabbed a stack of papers which she balanced on one arm, negotiated her coat and bag with the other and left the office. Erica watched her zigzag down the corridor until the inevitable dropping of the papers and personal effects occurred on cue by the lift. Under normal circumstances Erica would have been both amused and rushing to help, but the guilt she felt at thinking she'd been rumbled drove her to turn her head to work and a soulless lunch break welded to her desk.

By three o'clock, weary from the deprivation of having skipped lunch, Erica sought the company of her best friend at work, Carmi Mills. They sat together at the back of a stuffy panelled lecture theatre, pens poised, large paper cups filled with frothy coffee to hand. Evidenced by a ceiling covered in stained polystyrene tiles, the room had been renovated in the Sixties. A thin dado rail divided the walls into sections of eggshell blue and a dismal mid green. Oak desks and worn leather-cushioned benches cut into rigid panels were steeply tiered, the absence of any natural light leaving the expectant student cold.

"I've always hated this room." Said Erica. "Remind me why I'm here."

"You needed a break."'

"Ah. And there's me thinking you were up for a bit of a skive."

Carmi grinned, her dark lips pursed and eyes wide. "No such luck today sweet pea. I'm here to take notes. Between us, we should catch it all."

Erica shuffled on the narrow bench, crossing and uncrossing her legs in the restricted space. "Presumably this woman is published. Can't you just read one of her papers?"

"Yes, I guess so. But this is new stuff and she might be quite interesting."

"You could have just brought a tape recorder."

"That's a bit detached isn't it? I wouldn't have you as *my* secretary."

"I'm *not* a secretary."

"I'm joking." Carmi nudged Erica gently in the side. "It's good to see you flower."

"And you." Erica smiled and sucked at the froth on her latte creating a white moustache for her friend to see. "G'us a kiss."

The seminar convenor coughed to get silence and introduced the speaker and the title of the lecture: *Advances in luteinising hormone-releasing hormone agents*.

"Oh Christ," breathed Erica. "This is going to be terminal."

The speaker moved to the lectern and poked frustratedly at a laptop in order to get some presentation slides to operate. She was tall and slim with large scared-looking eyes and a pile of red hair that was no more stylish than a short back and sides.

"Why are scientists always such geeks?" Whispered Carmi. "I mean look at her – she's half way to Beaker from the Muppets."

Erica's nostrils flared and she stifled a laugh.

"I manage to be normal." Continued Carmi. "Why can't she? I bet she hasn't even got a handbag. Probably just some kind of satchel filled with litmus paper and baby wipes."

A student sitting in front of them turned and frowned at Carmi for the interruption. She moved her head forward and frowned back, inches from his face.

The lecture started and the pair settled back to take notes.

"Prostate cancer is the most common cancer in men in the UK and numbers have been rising steadily over the last twenty years. Even though there have been huge increases in cases diagnosed, the mortality rate has remained unchanged due to improvements in detection techniques. As a disease primarily found in older men and with the elderly population expected to increase over the next two decades, numbers are expected to continue to rise. Coupled with earlier diagnosis and increased detection rates, we can expect to be treating very large numbers of men in the future. Research into effective treatments and screening programmes has, not surprisingly, been on the up and I'm here today to talk about my work in this area, specifically around the effects of luteinising hormone-releasing hormone agents, or LHRH for short.

LHRH agonists act to suppress the production of testosterone in the male—"

Carmi yawned. "I could do with some of that for Reuben."

"What?" Whispered Erica.

"Some testosterone suppression. You would have thought that after twelve months of marriage he would have calmed down a bit, but oh no." Carmi sipped her coffee. "Honestly Erica, I'm knackered all the time. I'll order some LHRH and put it in his tea. I might get an uninterrupted night's sleep then."

Erica faced her friend and put her fingers in her ears. "Too much information." She mouthed.

Carmi scribbled in a battered notebook and Erica leant back, shifting again to get comfortable.

"— as has been for the treatment of prostate cancer, the LHRH agonists are just as effective as the removal of the testicles. This was once the standard treatment for the disease as testosterone can encourage the growth of prostate cancer cells and is produced primarily in that part of the body.

With the increased use of more aggressive therapies based around LHRH agonists, my research has been to examine some of the more severe side effects..."

Erica looked past the speaker and to the screen showing a projected image of a chart with increasingly-sized bars against an axis of time. She tilted her head to rest on the bench behind and relaxed quickly into a shallow sleep.

Carmi nudged her. "We can go now. C'mon, you heard her."

"What?"

"She just said that her lecture notes are going to be posted on the website. I can get everything there." She hesitated to take in Erica's tired face. "You've been asleep for almost half an hour. C'mon, we can get more coffee in the refectory."

Carmi, well-used to Erica's undulating enthusiasm for playing truant, kept the conversation at a steady pace as they got comfortable again in the canteen.

"I've been hearing about those burglaries in Brenly." She said.

"Attacks. Assaults." Corrected Erica eying the main entrance from their table. "Yeah... oh god, there's Alice from my corridor." She pulled her coat from the back of her chair. "I ought to go."

"No you don't. Sit down. For heaven's sake girl, she's probably having a break herself. You are allowed to stop for ten minutes you know."

"I kipped in the earth sciences library this morning and I've just spent half an hour sleeping through one of your lectures." Erica lowered herself back into her seat. "I'd fire me if I was Anita."

"So is it a local man?" Carmi persisted.

"Oh, I don't know." Erica was still looking over to the door.

"Right." Carmi paused. "You seem pretty laid back. I mean if there was some nutter going round breaking in to houses and punching old ladies in my area I'd be a little bit worried."

"Oh. Well no old ladies. A woman I think – a nurse and another woman in her house – disturbed him nicking stuff. But not on my street. Brenly's quite big you know. And, no one died." Erica looked at her friend over the table and Carmi frowned back theatrically, shrugging her shoulders. She was smart in a tight green roll neck with short sleeves, alert, enquiring; her dark skin smooth and moisturised.

"Well, as long as your calm approach to this isn't putting you in any danger."

Erica struggled to respond. In her attempt to sound causal she had, in her view, over-reacted. Providing a balanced commentary vexed her and to a certain degree, crept into the edges of paranoia. She shifted in her seat.

"I'm serious Erica. It must be difficult for you. I'm guessing. I mean, tell me it's none of my business, but it must be rattling the ghosts in the Ford family closet."

"You mean, my closet."

"Well yes." Carmi reached out across the table and took Erica's hand. "Have you told anyone else yet? Does Duncan know what happened to you?"

Erica pulled her hand back swiftly. "No!"

"OK, OK. Sorry."

Erica sighed. "No, I'm sorry."

The two sat in silence for a few moments and then went to speak at the same time.

"I can't –"

"I thought –"

Carmi smiled awkwardly and pulled her chair in closer. She spoke quietly, warmth in her voice. "I'll say no more, but if you're not confiding in Duncan, you can always talk to me. Assuming no one else knows."

"Thank you." Erica took a last swig of coffee and wiped her mouth with the back of her hand. "It was a long time ago, and I'm not going to get het up about it now. Burglaries are different anyway, you know. It's just, you know, it's just… the fear..."

Carmi nodded.

"I'm more worried for dad than for me." Her tone was unconvincing and Carmi arched a disbelieving eyebrow.

Erica stood up. "I really ought to go Carmi. Thanks for meeting up." She leant in to kiss her friend and to hug her awkwardly, head to head. "Lovely to see you as ever. And you look stunning in that top."

At five, Erica took the short journey to the outskirts of town to the brewery where Harry worked. She gave a cursory greeting to the security guard at the gates and headed up to her father's office. The building was empty for the day and she peered over the viewing gallery onto the brewery floor. Her father was prostate underneath the one of the vast copper kettles, with a bag of tools by his side and two of the brewers watching over him.

Erica paused to take in the heavy bready smell of the fermentation tanks in full flow and to watch the sweeping waves of creamy foam that spilled out from them. Her coat had fallen off one shoulder and a lock of hair lay undisturbed over one eye. The building was a simple oblong of Cotswold stone, the offices on a higher level overlooking the factory floor. Erica leant her chin on the heavy oak banister until she was eventually spotted by one of the brewers who prodded Harry for his attention. He peered out from under the kettle and looked up.

"I'll be up in five." He called back over the hum of machinery.

Erica's eyes flicked down to her father and she smiled kindly turning to amble back into the offices with half her coat trailing on the carpet. She threw her bag onto an old leather sofa in the reception area and extracted an insipid-looking hot chocolate from the vending machine. Pulling a copy of *Today's Scientist* from her bag she flicked through the week's news, her eyes coming to rest on a piece about a study of men in prison.

A paper published in the Journal of Biology and Behaviour is being held to question by authorities in Brazil. The paper reported research that revealed that fifteen out of twenty-five men who were castrated in order to calm them down went on to die. This was as a result of violent attacks on them in prison: the men, convicted violent criminals, were unable to defend themselves.

Men convicted of excessively violent crime are known to have higher levels of testosterone than average and the castration was performed as part of a study to reduce their violent behaviour. An inquest is under way to determine how many of the dead men actually consented to take part in the research. Their families are pressing charges against the researchers and the ethics of the study have left the courts divided.

"Should have given them some LHRH instead." Said Erica aloud.

Harry emerged up the stairs from the brewery floor, brushing down his overalls. "Pardon love?"

Erica looked up from her magazine. "Nothing."

He spent a few moments taking in his daughter's face. "Are you OK love? You look like you've seen a ghost."

"No I'm fine." Said Erica, forcing a weak smile.

Harry nodded and disappeared into his office. "I'm just going to get changed and then I'll be with you." He called out. "Thanks for picking me up love. Frank's had the car since lunch but it needs a few parts to get it through the service. He'll have to have it tomorrow too..." Harry ventured.

"S'OK. No problem." Erica's voice was low, distracted.

She looked out past her father's office, her eyes moving along the floorboards via strips of orange sunlight cast through the narrow sash windows. She stood up slowly, absently letting the magazine slide off her lap and moved with the pace of someone feeling their way in the dark, tracing the line of her own gaze out onto the viewing gallery.

Harry, overalls crumpled on the floor, was leafing through a thick lever arch file in his office and sipping from a half empty glass of beer. Erica walked past without glancing in.

"I'm having problems locating some paperwork that I need for my trip."

"What trip?"

"I'm off to Norwich to pick up some yeast next week and I was thinking of staying over."

"Oh." She stopped for a moment. "Why can't they send it down dad, and why do you always go up there to collect it?"

"Oh I don't mind love. It's nice to see the chaps up there and we're having a meeting too, probably with dinner afterwards. You know how it is."

"Right."

Erica moved out into the viewing gallery and stopped. She panned the brewery floor, taking in the brightly lit equipment and the clashing odours of cleaning fluid and fermentation. A stack of empty metallic beer barrels stood at one end of the floor, ready for filling when the current brew had finished.

"You'll miss the talk in Brenly by the police. That's tomorrow night too you know." She offered quietly.

Harry didn't appear to hear.

She frowned, scratching her head, her hair messy and greasy at the roots. The only sound was the hum of a single tank beneath her, spewing foam in steady pulses. It was a view she had taken in a hundred times and she hunkered down to take hold of the balusters, pressing her face between them. Her eyes flicked from the empty barrels to a line of barley sacks, white nylon and bulging, to the room-sized mash tubs and finally to the engineering spectacle that were the two enormous copper kettles. They stood like cartoon space rockets at the end of the factory, bolted and welded cylindrical beasts with conical lids standing thirty feet high.

Erica stared at them for several moments, motionless.

At the sound of her father's footsteps approaching the platform she stood up quickly and caught her head on the railing.

"Mind love." Said Harry holding out wiry hands and taking hold of her head for a moment. He ruffled her hair and placed a light kiss on her forehead.

"Yoda's fixed." Harry waved down to point at the fermentation tanks that lined the wall beneath the viewing gallery.

"Anakin and Leia have just been given the all clear. All being well we'll be back to full capacity by the weekend."

Erica caught the pride in his voice that always came when the brewery was restored somehow after periods of breakdown or a slack in trade.

"Yeah." She muttered, walking slowly behind him back in to the offices.

She turned before extinguishing the gallery lights and looked back once more into the brewery, small beads of sweat forming on her upper lip.

FOUR

It was the end of a sunless, rainless, nothingness of a winter, followed by a springtime of rain. Erica rested her chin on the windowsill in her office and looked over to the car park through a veil of water, people streaming like ants at the end of the day.

Harry, leaving no room for guesswork as to his agenda, had left a scribbled note that morning urging Erica to stay at Duncan's or go into town to meet friends in his absence. The desperate overtones in his instructions for Erica to move through her twenties with a lighter step, appeared to make no dent in her motivations.

She picked up the phone and called Duncan at his desk explaining the need to spend the night with him.

"A month ago I wouldn't have cared. But it's different at the moment. Dad said he's worried about me being on my own and he thought it'd be a good idea." Erica spoke quietly into the phone.

"Fine by me. Though I'd rather you came to stay at mine." Said Duncan.

"Why?"

"Because Andy and I are installing a network in the flat tonight and it may take some time."

"A network?"

"Yes, it means we can connect our computers together."

"Jesus Duncan. Spare me. Why do you need an evening to network two computers? You both work in IT for Christ's sake."

"OK, OK. Well, it's not that simple. We want to play this new game and it doesn't work so well over wi-fi. So it's more of a wiring job, get the cabling sorted once and for all. And well, we wanted to test it all out."

Erica remained silent.

"Really Erica, it's very good. Amazing in fact…" He trailed off.

"You can play games on the console."

"You don't get it." Duncan paused. "Let's just leave it there." He concluded with an edge to his voice.

Erica leant on her desk and rested her forehead in her free hand. "I don't get *you* more like."

"What? That's not fair. Had I known you needed me tonight I'd have kept it free. You're hardly flattering me with your reasons to spend the night together. I'm just a convenience because your dad doesn't want you to be alone in the house." He paused. "Now, if you'd said 'Duncan, I want your hot Scottish body, be over at eight', that would have been different."

"Duncan!" Hissed Erica. "I assume there's people in your office that can hear you."

Duncan laughed quietly. "Maybe. But I am serious; you'll have to come over to mine. I don't know when I'll be finished. You might even have to watch two sweaty boys in clashing avatars fight to the death. Except that, well… Andy usually likes to play as a woman."

"You're just trying to get a rise out of me." Erica glanced furtively up the corridor. "OK. I'll be over around nine. I'm going to this talk first. And please sort your room out before I get there."

Erica closed her office door, sat back at her desk biting her nails for a moment. She Googled 'testosterone, aggression' on her computer.

A result of several hundred possible links appeared on her screen and she skimmed through the first few pages.

…men who have been convicted of violent crimes… higher levels of testosterone … violent lifestyle leads to high testosterone… aggressive encounters…

"Blah blah blah." Said Erica aloud and entered 'LHRH manufacturer'.

A short list of papers, pharmaceutical manufacturers and cancer charity websites appeared. She honed in on a product manufactured in India and scanned the details of the company producing it.

... LHRH has different brand names in different countries and may be sold by different companies... we supply the health service in several Asian and European countries... special arrangements for research units... collaboration with medical schools in universities in Delhi and Bangalore...

Erica followed a link to the page for 'Enquiries and ordering' and sat back. In order to place an order there were mandatory fields that needed to be completed including a return address. She typed in her name, credit card details and email but entered Carmi's department as postal address. She pondered over the free text box explaining the nature of her enquiry for several minutes, writing and rewriting a short message.

The sound of the cleaners in the corridor made no impact on Erica's consciousness and when her office door opened abruptly some moments after completing her message, she screamed, quickly and at high pitch.

"Sorry." The cleaner held up her hand and reversed out of the room pulling the nozzle of the vacuum cleaner behind her.

Erica put her hand to her heart at the shock of being disturbed. She reached for her coat and bag looking back at the text she had entered into the enquiry form blinking at her from the screen. After another minute or so of staring at it, she lurched forward, clicked to send the message and stepped back, gasping at her own action, her hand over her mouth.

"Are we all in?" The police officer boomed from the front of the hall. "There's a few more chairs down this end."

He ushered some latecomers to the front and made a jokes about troublemakers always choosing to sit at the back.

His apparent conviviality at an event billed with such serious overtones caused a few brows to lower.

Three police officers and a couple of the parish councillors dressed in ill-fitting tweed jackets sat at the front of the hall behind a trestle table. Artwork from the children's playgroup dotted the walls and flanking the length of the room were notice boards awash with details of blood donation clinics, jumble sales and public transport timetables. Hefty iron radiators thick with decades of repainting, pumped out heat into the already stuffy room.

It had taken a fraction of the village's residents to turn up for the hall to be filled and the session began to a backdrop of the shuffling of feet of latecomers on the dusty floor. Erica was among them. She leant against a wall and picked at a bag of chips, the odour pleasantly over-riding a stale breeze of modelling clay and rubber gymnastic mats. Having half a mind on the introductions that were taking place and half on emptying the contents of the bag as quickly as possible, she finished the chips swiftly and squeezed the paper bag into a tight roll, stuffing it with some force into her pocket. Looking up, her face was a statement of renewed interest – *Here I am. What's going on?* – and met the eyes of the same police officer that had visited her house. He passed her a shy smile and looked back at his notes in front of him.

Erica felt her ears burning. She pulled her hair down over them and looked out from under her black crown, eyes widened and attentive. The lead detective described in detail, more vivid than had been reported by the press, the precise injuries sustained by those who had been attacked in their homes and the similarities between them. The victims' ordeals had been thankfully short-lived and no permanent physical damage would be sustained by any of them.

Erica burped and at once felt relieved from the mounting pressure that had been building during the detective's diatribe. She swigged from a bottle of water and paled as vividly as she had previously blushed, hugging the wall more closely as the details were delivered.

It was revealed that the burglar had had an anger about him that had frightened those whom he had disturbed. He had grunted but not spoken and so no regional accent was discernable. The detective went on to describe what was known of his physical appearance and passed round a crude photo-fit.

Motives were discussed, the time that had elapsed between the incidents and then the final blow – that despite the lack of any discernable identification of his voice, they were most likely to be looking for a local person – possibly as local as Brenly itself.

A murmur rose about the room as the audience were left to digest these comments for a few moments. The detective broke the hubbub by reminding them to remain vigilant, follow some basic guidance as to home security and report any suspicious behaviour immediately. The officers took questions and Erica detected a certain briskness in the responses given. She herself felt some disappointment in the format of the presentation insofar as there were more questions in her mind when it was over than when she had arrived. Faked smiles of camaraderie were passed between neighbours though the hall did not empty quickly and people loitered to speak to the police and to each other.

Erica slunk to the toilets, brushed her hair and applied a dab of lip balm. She buttoned her coat up to the neck in order to cover a shapeless grey jumper and moved quickly back into the main hall, making a beeline for the police officer she had recognised.

"Hello." Erica stood bold and upright and held out a stiff hand in greeting.

"Hello." He took her hand and shook it firmly.

"I'm Erica Ford and I'm doing some research at the –"

"We met the other week – you live in the Old Rectory."

They spoke over each other and came to a halt, still holding one another's hands.

The formality that Erica had planned to project on to the exchange gave way in seconds to the usual stammering awkwardness that plagued her social interactions with men of a similar age. She was relieved when he picked up from the fumbled introduction, in a broad Ulster accent.

"My name's Connor Fairchild. We met a while ago when I was doing my rounds. Sorry, you said your name was...?"

"Erica uh, Ford. Erica Ford."

"Nice to meet you. How can I help?"

Erica, still smiling, felt a wave of heat rising up her back and to her neck. She wanted desperately to unbutton her coat but was held back by an awareness of her own vanity in the moment and the desire to hide her clothing. Despite being drawn to Connor's warmth in what should have been a formal exchange, she wanted the conversation to end quickly.

"Sorry, you said something about research." He prompted.

"Oh yes, yes. I work at the university and am doing some research into local patterns of behaviour among certain groups, geographically speaking. And well, I was wondering if you could help me."

"Oh right, well, we've plenty of behavioural psychologists working with us, so perhaps I could put you in touch with someone." Connor offered brightly. "And there's me thinking you were about to congratulate us on such an engaging presentation."

His light blond hair was thinning and cut short and his pale skin was peppered with freckles. Erica was reminded of the time when she had met him on her doorstep in that she felt drawn to this man with an unmissably broad frame, which was counter to her usual shrinking mistrust of large men.

She swallowed and unbuttoned the top of her coat, unable to keep control of her rising body heat.

"Yes, yes, it was good, thank you. Well, not good, if you know what I mean, but very well done. You got the facts over." Erica stammered. "And I'm sure you'll find him soon enough. Can't think who in Brenly would suddenly start burglaring though. Is burglaring a word? Anyway, someone would have noticed something by now surely." Erica stopped short and noticed that Connor was still smiling at her.

"Well if you do notice anything, you'll be sure to get in touch." He added.

"Absolutely."

"You live with your parents in the Old Rectory, is that right?" Connor remained still, feet sturdy at a hip's width apart while Erica shuffled from one foot to the other.

"No, well yes, I do live there but just with my dad. I sort of, well, look after him in a way."

"Ah yes, when the tables turn and you find yourself looking after your parents. I know the story."
Erica was surprised to find Connor making small talk and was unsure as to how to reply.

"You'll not be going back there on your own now." Connor's smile levelled and he lowered his voice as if issuing concern for a friend. "You'll have company I hope."

"Oh I'm driving straight into town actually. I'm staying with um, uh, a friend." Erica's blush that had stayed lurking behind her ears until that point charged on to her face at this revelation.

She looked down at her feet for a moment to collect herself.

"Good, I'm glad to hear it. These incidents really have been nasty and we really do think it could be a local man. Short of collecting everyone's DNA, we're being as thorough as we can."

Erica kept her gaze down and considered the brevity with which she was entering into this exchange. He was a police officer, a detective possibly, working on a very serious case, and she was lying to him in order to attempt to obtain information under false pretences. She took a step back in preparation to depart and to abandon the dialog with her own sense of decency intact.

"So, do you want me to put you in touch with someone?" Asked Connor.

Erica looked at him earnestly and thought she might be sick as she considered her next words.

"Well no, but thank you all the same. Well, maybe, I don't know. It seems silly now that I ask."

"Right…" Connor gathered some leaflets and papers that were strewn on the table and stuffed them into a bulging case.

"It's not a behavioural psychologist I'm after. I'm looking for facts – statistics really. I'm a statistical sociologist."

"Oh, OK."

A statistical sociologist? Where in god's name …? She stumbled on. "And I was really looking for some information on crime statistics in this county, the city even, local figures…" She paused. "…over the next six to twelve months or so in relation to…" She wavered again. "…particular locations. Erm, I can't say much more than that at the moment because it's sort of, uh, confidential and uh, possibly controversial." She stopped and noticed that Connor was eyeing her with what appeared to be sincere interest, and not relative disbelief, which was what she was expecting.

"Well, there's rakes of information on crime and demographics that I could point you in the direction of, some of it more sensitive than others, obviously. A lot of it's already on the Internet."

"That would be great, thank you."

The hall was clearing and Erica became aware that the remaining police officers were shifting slowly towards the exit, one stopping to gesture to Connor and pointing to her wristwatch.

"Let me give you my number." Connor lowered his voice again, took out a pen and scribbled onto a piece of paper, handing it to Erica. It appeared to her to be a personal mobile number and she looked at him quizzically.

"Call me when you've figured out what you'd like to know and I'll see what I can dig out for you. Or for that matter, if you've anything to report on the recent incidents."

"Is this your – "

"That's my mobile, yes. Looks like I'm needed." He gestured to his colleagues and gave Erica a barely discernable wink as he departed.

FIVE

It is a view held by those who chose to ponder on the patterns of fate in life, that bad things will always happen in threes. Erica Ford had long held a version of this view that bad things generally occurred in clusters, sometimes threes, sometimes fours, separated by stagnant periods of treading water. Life, it seemed, was just as able to deliver pleasant surprises and it was unpleasant ones, even if the frequency of the latter far outweighed that of the former. Happier moments were unusual and rarely of her own creation and not to be anticipated or they would never follow. She believed however, that something would eventually happen in her life that would break this pattern she had grown to expect and accept, and somehow instil a permanently lighter edge to her existence. What that thing was that would change everything was not specific, but had been increasingly playing on her mind.

The revelation that *she* might need to be the one to exact the change upon her had been the occupying thought of the year so far, the catalyst for which had been the darker events that had taken place closer to home and the encounters with Connor Fairchild.

The day after the visit by the police to Brenly village hall, Erica had spent a difficult lunch break explaining to Carmi why she had had a package delivered from India in Carmi's name.

"It's pharmaceuticals. I'm not stupid." Was Carmi's indignant challenge.

"No it's not, it's a new fertilizer I'm trying in the garden. It's cheaper to order it from India than buy it here."

"Made from what? Tiger poo?"

"No. It's bat droppings. It's called, uh, guava."

Carmi had paused and sat back. "You mean *guano* Erica, it being a Spanish word. You find that stuff in South America."

"Yes, yes I know – *duh* – this is Indian guano, which is why it's so rare and unheard of in gardening circles. I'm going to give it a try."

"Well don't blow yourself up." They had been sitting in the refectory together and Carmi was becoming animated.

"What?"

"Nitrogen and phosphorus. You'll blow yourself up." She had stirred a pot of yogurt with its accompanying compote so vigorously that it had turned into a dark red goo.

"Oh, no. Of course not."

"So why have it sent in my name? Anita's hardly going to sack you for having something delivered to work."

"I just thought that, you know, substances would be better coming to Medicine than to my department. It might have been opened by Customs or something."

There had been silences between them and Carmi, despite finding Erica's explanation wholly unsatisfactory, had decided to let the subject drop. When Erica had eventually wrested the package from her friend's office she had made apologies to leave hastily and despatched the parcel to the boot of her car for the rest of the afternoon.

Professor Singh had been demanding for the remainder of the day and on returning home, Erica headed out immediately for a walk to clear her head. She strolled around the streets of the village to take in the last of the evening sunshine and kick up drifts of cherry blossom that had formed on the pavements. Her head down, she chewed over when and where she might unpack the parcel and decided to leave it where it was for the time being. The plan that was formulating in her head came to a halt when she turned the corner of an adjacent street and caught the strobe lights of emergency services vehicles. The driveway of one of the larger cottages in the village was host to several police cars and a dozen or so neighbours standing in clusters in the road.

Heaps of purple wisteria that pulled at the cottage's stone walls were pushed aside as people ducked their heads to move over the low threshold. Carefully kept flower beds were awkwardly negotiated by police officers in various uniforms and the word 'forensic' skittered through Erica's mind as she watched people mill about. Police officers took questions from the onlookers and their colleagues scratched about on the lawn, stooped and clutching clear plastic bags. Erica's legs continued to propel her nearer to the house and she made her way slowly towards one of the loitering groups of neighbours. A girl amongst them had been in her class at school and Erica touched her arm awkwardly as she joined her.

"Hi Jo."

"Oh hi Erica."

"What happened?"

"It was that nutter again. He got in and took a load of stuff from the bedrooms apparently. Jewellery, that kind of thing. The cleaner came by and found him in the house so he thumped her. She's in hospital now, concussed they said and not in great shape. Talking to the police no doubt."

"God that's awful." Said Erica staring over at the cottage. "How did he get in?"

"Not sure. I can't see any broken windows. Police said that there wasn't a forced entry. The family's on holiday at the moment so they're on their way back. All a bit strange if you ask me."

"So I take it he's gone — the burglar."

"Oh yeah. Big time. He legged it straight away out the back apparently but no one saw anything."

They both paused to stare back at the house, Erica straining to make out the faces of the police officers that were coming and going.

Jo turned to face Erica, hands thrust deep in a garish summer Macintosh. "You wanna be careful Erica."

"Eh?"

"Living in that big house. He's only gone for big ones round here, the nice-looking cottages, that kinda thing. You still live in the rectory with your dad don't you?"

"Yeah." Erica's voice was a whisper and she shuffled to and fro for a moment on the loose tarmac. "I better go. Thanks Jo. I'm going to call dad now." The pair exchanged half smiles in parting and Erica headed back down the street.

Harry was waiting for her in the driveway when she arrived.

"I'm glad you're here love, I was about to pop out and get a pint."

"Thanks for waiting." Said Erica, panting from a fast walk.

She rested her head against his neck and welcomed his tight hug on the doorstep. They moved in to the house, Harry ushering her in to join him for a glass of beer in the lounge. They sat together quietly picking through the information she had of the latest break-in. Harry was keen to remind Erica that on each occasion the burglar must have thought that he was entering an empty house; Erica was quick to point out that he had got it wrong every time.

"Don't worry love." Harry had continued. "We're very secure here – no one could get past our locks and most of the sash windows are nailed down now. Besides, there's nothing really to steal."

Erica passed an eye around the windows in the room.

"In broad daylight. That's the thing that gets me." Mused Harry. "Still, we'll be sure to leave plenty of lights on Saturday night when we're both out."

Erica looked at her father quizzically.

"It's the ball – at the brewery." Said Harry.

Erica closed her eyes and sipped slowly from her glass.

Third crap thing: lied to my best friend, nutter strikes again, brewery bloody ball. What's the fourth?

"Yeah, of course. Sorry. Forgot for a moment then. For some reason I thought it was next weekend."

"First Saturday in May love." Harry squinted at a line of remote controls laid out on the coffee table. He picked one up staring at it closely, turned it one hundred and eighty degrees and aimed it at the television. "Same every year." He went on. "Not so much a ball this year though as just a bit of a party – no black tie, though we've got a swing band booked."

"No black tie? I've told Duncan to hire a suit – no. Don't worry." Erica interrupted herself. "It'll do him good."

They settled into watching the evening news, Harry engrossed, Erica's eyes flicking about the room, not concentrating until she had finished her beer.

She stood up and collected Harry's glass from him.

"Nothing to steal dad?"

Harry was still staring at the television.

"Apart from a laptop, two TVs, stereos, all that silver, mum's jewellery, your art stuff." She paused for a moment. "Oh, and three shotguns, lest we forget." She concluded.

"S'mostly junk love." Harry said weakly.

Erica shook her head and padded out of the room.

The guilt that Erica felt for having lied so comprehensively to Carmi, combined with the news of the latest burglary, made for a restless night in the Old Rectory. Erica had watched the clock until the early morning and listened to her father potter to and from the bathroom during the night. She had spent time sitting at the top of the stairs taking in the clutter of the old house, enjoying the contours cast by the moon's bleak illumination: every shelf and surface was a place for a clock, an ornament or a pile of papers. The walls were filled with large gilt-framed canvases of still life, ponds in the style of Monet and flowers arranged in china vases on crinkled white tablecloths, evidence of a lifetime's hobby that was Harry's. They lined the hallway and the staircase and were present in every room, including the kitchen.

The tiredness did not come and she taken to laying on her back in the spare room, her arm resting over her forehead to block moonlight and then dawn light from her eyes. It never normally bothered her, but on bad nights the light that seeped around the curtains seemed to be as bright as day.

When at last she settled into a light sleep her thoughts drifted to the brewery, its uneven concrete floors, hoppers, pipes and taps. She saw Harry move in and out of focus checking his watch, tapping and taking readings from dials. She saw herself mount the spiral metal steps up the side of one of the great copper kettles. Wearing denim flares and a t-shirt with a print of yellow fish, her hair falling down to her waist in uneven curls as it had done as a teenager, she stooped to keep a hold of the collar of her old dog Jack who sat by her on the raised platform at the top of the kettle. They looked back down the length of the building, eyes resting on the figure of a tall, well-built man in a police uniform, feet hip-width apart, looking back at them.

By eight she was awake again and sent a text to Carmi to see if she was free for a visit. Erica had considered long into the night that the only way to make herself feel better about her dishonesty was to seek Carmi's advice on an unrelated matter. It was a transparent attempt to appease her guilt and one that Carmi would undoubtedly see through immediately. Nevertheless, a fracture in their friendship would be repaired and Carmi was quick to respond.

Erica was standing in Carmi's front room by ten o'clock wearing a long yellow dress that she had borrowed from Janice.

"What do you think? This or my standard black number?" Erica asked.

Carmi raised her eyebrows.

"Seriously Carmi, I need your advice. Is this a mistake?"

"Put the black one on."

Erica slipped out of her sister's dress and into a square-necked black pencil dress that had been her staple for every wedding, funeral and brewery ball for the past five years.

"You see, white girls really shouldn't wear yellow." Began Carmi dully. "Least of all lemon yellow. Unless you've got whiter than white teeth, the observer is immediately drawn to notice that you've inadvertently coordinated your teeth to match your outfit. The one brings out the colour of the other. So, in my opinion, definitely the black one even though the neckline is *so* last decade. You need to get yourself to the shops today and find something altogether different. *Or*." Carmi paused. "Get some accessories – red ones – a belt and some shoes, and have your hair down, but really big it up." She waved her arms around her head to demonstrate the expansion possibilities of Erica's hair.

"Right." Erica smiled. It was what she loved about Carmi. She had a way of putting things honestly without causing offence. "But Janice's dress is Versace. Well. Eighties Versace."

"Then why are you asking me for my opinion? No – don't answer that." Carmi smiled at her friend. "Seriously, unless you get an invite to a fancy dress party where the theme is spring flowers, you should just let it go. Obviously I'm pleased that at last you're asking me for my opinion and that years of me dropping hints has finally paid off…" Carmi shook her head. "But twenty-year old Versace? You really are in the land that time forgot when it comes to dress sense sometimes."

"Cheers." Said Erica. "And I've got yellow teeth as well it seems."

"For god's sake woman, that's not what I meant. You've got a terrific figure but you just wear these dreadful get-ups."

"Dreadful?" Erica looked down at the dress and smoothed the fabric around her hips.

Carmi clapped her hands signalling a conclusion to the debate. "Wear the black one tonight. You can borrow a belt and bag off me if you like. On one condition."

Erica looked up.

"You tell me what was in that package."

Erica's heart sank and she fiddled with the zip on her dress. To tell Carmi the truth would require an explanation that Erica herself had not fully entertained. She was dabbling with ideas only; no physical act of meddling had taken place, nothing was written down and her hands were not yet soiled. It was all loosely connected strings of cause and effect, maybes and what ifs; no concrete timetable of action, just a simmering rage for the inequalities of life that had propelled her thus far into her plan for the spring time of her twenty-sixth year.

Carmi sighed and sank back into the sofa. "Forget it. Just messing." She was unconvincing. "You let me take you shopping next week and we sort your wardrobe out."

Erica took no time to consider her response and agreed to Carmi's suggestion. Despite having marginally more interest in shopping for clothes than Duncan, she considered that the activity would more than placate her mounting guilt for holding back from her friend.

By six o'clock that evening she was slinking about the house in a pair of Carmi's red shoes, closing doors and switching on lights with crimson-painted fingernails and hair blow-dried into spectacular curves. The doorbell rang as Erica was throwing a lipstick and comb into a bag.

"That'll be Duncan. I'll get it." She called to her father and clumped gingerly downstairs.

"I'll be two minutes." Harry shouted back from the bathroom.

"Uh!" She groaned, pulling the door from its swollen frame.

Connor Fairchild was standing on the doorstep. He was in uniform, radio buzzing intermittently from his lapel, his hat tucked under his arm.

"Hi." He said.

"Hi." Said Erica. "We, uh, dad and me are just off out. Um, so uh yeah, so I can't invite you in." Erica could feel her heart beating increasingly heaving blows against her ribcage.

"Yes, I see. Not to worry. I'm just calling to see that everything's OK here."

"Yes fine."

"And to let you know that there'll be a few more police officers about than normal this evening and tomorrow." Connor's voice wavered slightly with this explanation and for the first time Erica wondered if it was his turn to be guilty of making things up as he went along. She heard the sound of a car engine whine in deceleration and looked anxiously past him into the road.

"Right, well, as long as everything's OK…" Said Connor stepping down on to the gravel. "You'll be sure to get in touch if you see anything suspicious."

"Yes, yes I will." It hurt Erica to respond so curtly but her anxiety for Duncan appearing at that same moment was greater.

"Well, have a good evening."

A river of air, thick with spring perfume, whipped Erica's hair off her face and pushed the fabric of her dress tight against her body. She stood in the doorway looking back at Connor, eyes squinting in the breeze, as he marched purposefully down the drive. He glanced back and his path meandered for a moment as he acknowledged Erica on the doorstep and tipped his hat in farewell.

SIX

Harry had been at the brewery his entire working life. The first five years of his apprenticeship was served while his own father worked the delivery yard. His ascent to wealth far beyond the means of a brewer's apprentice came in the form of his courtship with Dorothy Hunter, the daughter of a ship-building entrepreneur who had curiously retired to land-locked Oxfordshire. Dorothy was the only child of her father's second marriage and when both her parents died in a ferry disaster (on a boat which, ironically, was constructed in one of her father's shipyards) Dorothy inherited the old Cotswold stone rectory in Brenly-on-Thames that she had grown up in. As a woman of twenty years she was old enough to take care of the place herself and clung to it and all its sagging stone work in her grief.

Harry too lost his father at that time, the family doctor claiming that alcohol had destroyed his liver and that if Harry had any sense he'd leave the brewery immediately and the deadly temptations it afforded. Dorothy and Harry, despite the scorn of Dorothy's parents when they had been alive, had been courting for a year by that time and were drawn closer in their shared grief. They married six months later and Harry moved in to the Old Rectory.

They had a modest wedding. Dorothy's half siblings, who had inherited the business wealth of the their shared father, deigned to show their faces at the ceremony, leaving swiftly afterwards in a spin of Jaguars and Aston Martin saloons. Dorothy wore her hair down, and floated around the house dressed in a smock-like cream dress, loosely beaded, and smoked marijuana in the greenhouse with Harry while guests arrived from the church. She was secretly vexed at the unabashed glee with which her new mother-in-law gloated at her son's match with such an apparently wealthy young woman, crediting herself to have encouraged Harry to mix with the upper classes in the city at weekends.

Although she welcomed her mother-in-law into the house in the years that followed, Dorothy worked hard to hide her relief when she died suddenly from pneumonia a decade later. She had noted to Harry that the crazy old bat was prone to offering cigarettes to the children at the end of the garden.

The truth was that Harry differed from his siblings in a way that estranged him from them to a larger extent throughout his life. He was an obsessive reader and tended towards science texts. It was unquestioned that he should leave school at fifteen and take on an apprenticeship, but after a joyless summer on the Austin Morris production line, he moved to the brewery. The frustrations of an eager chemist were finally sated with a lifetime of tinkering with hops, malts and yeasts, mash temperatures and fermentation times.

Marrying Dorothy gave Harry a direction and a motivation he embraced bodily, and the hope that he might migrate to the social circles he craved. Dorothy herself had bagged a working class boy and had filled the void that was left by her family. Whilst the house itself was worth a great deal of money, there was no other element to Dorothy's inheritance and the couple's joint salary was the only income to keep the old place reasonably maintained. After a particularly stormy winter that saw roof tiles fall in abundance and damp rise through the floor, they argued for months over whether to sell the place and move to somewhere altogether more manageable: Dorothy was passionate that it was all she had left of her parents while Harry resented spending his free time in overalls. It was only when business picked up at the brewery and Harry's status elevated with it, were they able to employ tradesmen to repair and renovate their home.

To Ellen and Erica, the constant toing and froing between bedrooms to avoid domestic disruption, was part of the joy of their childhood. It seemed natural to them to always be on the move in a place that had a dozen rooms on both floors and an acre of garden. Janice was the less tolerant of the three and would spend nights in her room with buckets laid to catch water, bed pushed up against a wall and toys arranged under a line of umbrellas.

The beers that Harry engineered as a young man had stayed in demand for decades and he had persuaded the owners to allow him to put much of the profit back into the business. He commissioned the replacement of the brewery's floundering equipment with solid, traditional models; he renovated the offices, staff facilities and adjacent pub. He expanded the factory floor by just enough to double output to please the investors while keeping the premises small enough to maintain a manageable empire.

It was a small team that ran the brewery, dedicated and involved. Everybody knew everyone's business to the extent that Harry's peers suspected that he had craved a son to continue the working tradition in his family. The rumour was that the reason he had taken on so many shifts when Erica was born was not because he had another mouth to feed, but because he was so disappointed that she was a girl and preferred to be away from home in the early days of her life.

The speculation was true enough. The closeness between Erica and Harry was eventually formed through an alliance based on neediness and guilt and set Erica apart from her sisters when Dorothy had died. Erica had been born a full eight years after Ellen and Harry observed that while she evidently loved her older sisters, she could never truly break into their bond. He hoped that she contented herself with the knowledge that whilst their mother was gone, she had Harry to herself and that that was good enough. It was a force that kept her living at home well into her twenties.

The ball was, as it always was, a success. Erica sipped from a gin and tonic from the sidelines and took it all in. Whilst she was fond of the brewery staff, she considered the balls to be something of an endurance test when it came to answering relentless but well-meaning enquiries. They key to a stress-free evening was drink enough gin early on and then pace herself with water and wine.

She observed her family tackle the challenge: Ellen and Francoise making headway through the guests as skilled and interested enquirers, rarely ever more than a metre apart from each other; even Janice, with her precise choreography to remain steadfastly in opposite corners to Harry at all times and who made blithe excuses to leave early, parted with flushed cheeks and a light step. There they were, these siblings that tiptoed around her, shielding her from god knows what, though always protective with one eye on their fragile little sis.

Erica sought out Duncan. She had observed in him the ability to latch on to men with an IT bent and had twice pulled him away from the bar that evening to dance, considering her moves to free others from his focussed diatribes as merciful acts. On this last occasion, instead of trying to explain to Erica what he had been discussing with his most recent bar fellow, he surprised her.

"If you had the choice of six limbs, what would you rather have — two arms and four legs or four arms and two legs?" He shouted in to Erica's ear.

She rolled her eyes and her drift from sobriety allowed her to nod her head against his shoulder.

"If I had six limbs, I'd be an insect." She hollered back.

"Don't be a pedant. C'mon. You're a mammal, make your choice."

"OK. If I was a predator then I'd go for two legs and four arms, but if I was prey, then I'd go for four legs and two arms, maybe even just six legs, then I could get away quickly."

"Six legs isn't an option."

"Fine. Four legs it is. Or three of each. Is that allowed?"

"No. Physiological impossibility."

"OK. Four legs then."

"Go on."

"Well I dunno now I come to think of it. If I *did* have four arms then I could multi-task much more easily. I could make dinner with two arms, a phone call with another and have a spare one for emergencies." She stopped moving and held Duncan by the shoulders. "You could programme two computers at once – just think! You'd be in your element."

"Or I'd be redundant. There'd be twice as much programming potential on the planet."

Erica was laughing. It was almost the last endearing trait about Duncan — his ability to generate imagined consequences with enduring seriousness.

He went on. "But if having four arms *did* allow for much greater multi-tasking, how would the brain cope? I don't think it would do so well in its current form. People would be knitting and driving at the same time and there'd be crashes everywhere. We'd need much better developed frontal lobes if we were to cope with four arms."

"What? No." Erica shook her head emphatically. "For a start, if we did evolve to have more arms, the brain would evolve at the same rate. And anyway, the frontal lobe is for behaviour and stuff we learn. It's your cerebral *hemispheres* that would need more development." Erica was triumphant and looked Duncan in the eyes as steadily as she could, happy to be in territory he could not dispute.

"OK, but we're agreed then that these celestial hemispheres would need to be more developed then to cope with having four arms?"

"Most definitely."

"So, extrapolating from that then, you're saying that the bigger a brain is, the more function it can have?" Duncan had his eyes closed, swaying out of time to the beat.

"I'm not walking into that one Duncan." Erica was quick to retaliate. "Development and complexity does not necessarily equate to greater size. My sister's the biggest feminist on the planet and she'd eat you for breakfast if she heard you say what I think you're about to say."

Duncan held up his hand. "I never said anything about the size of women's brains compared to men's. Except when it comes to parking a car – the carparkus campus is definitely smaller in women's brains than in men's."

It was a poorly considered cliché and Erica shook her head disappointedly.

"Under normal circumstances I would walk away from anyone that dealt such a shallow and pathetic blow, but on this occasion, I need you to stick with me." Erica was barely making an effort to dance now. Duncan's drift into hackneyed stereotyping reminded her of the rise and fall in her feelings for him.

"But do you need me to stick with you for more than just tonight?"

"What?"

"Do you need me to stick with—"

"I heard you. What do you mean?"

Duncan stepped nearer to his girlfriend and bellowed in her ear. "I mean, are you happy? With me."

The chorus of the song being played brought with it spontaneous accompaniment from the dance floor. Duncan continued over the elevated noise. "You've been a bit distracted lately especially with me and I wasn't sure if it was the whole burglary thing, or your mum, or if it was us. I mean, me."

The song ended abruptly and the last of Duncan's words were projected clumsily onto the dance floor.

"Fantastic." He whispered and led Erica away. "Sorry. I didn't anticipate that very well did I?"

Erica leant against the bar, her back to the glittering dance floor. The band picked up with a mellower beat. "It's OK. And I'm OK. Really I'm fine. Though I have been a bit distracted. It's probably the burglary stuff."

"You're sure?"

She picked at a bowl of peanuts. "Yeah. Think so. Why?"

"Well, now that you ask, I've sort of booked us a little holiday thing, something to cheer you up, get you away from big bad Brenly."

"Oh. Wow."

"We're going to Barcelona for the weekend in two week's time. There's a Gaudi festival so it should be extra specially fun."

Erica put her arms inside Duncan's jacket and cupped a handful of flab in each hand. He beamed at her and pushed his glasses back up his round and sweaty nose.

Erica playfully squeezed Duncan's sides with her hands. In an instant she had calculated that the excursion might be a useful measure to gauge her true affection: if they drifted into arguments over an intense period of only two days together, they would inevitably be confronted with the mortality of their relationship. And if they *did* reach this conclusion about their own compatibility, there was at least the upside of seeing the *Sagrada Familia* again. If they went their separate ways, Duncan would be bound to bounce back quickly, their friendship intact, and Erica would be free to pursue possibilities with Connor. As someone that had spent most of her adult life single, this final element to her own internal peremptory conclusion on the matter excited her.

"Thanks D. You're so sweet sometimes. I totally don't deserve you. It *would* be really good to get away for a bit."

"Ah… thank god. I had Andy on stand by in case you said no, but he's far too hairy to share a bed with."

It was the following weekend before Erica removed the package from the boot of her car. She had risen early with Harry before he had left for a Saturday shift and had surprised him with her attentiveness. They made plans for the garden over breakfast sitting outside in the morning sun, noting new clumps of foxgloves among the ferns and the brilliance of the bluebells. Harry mused, as he did every year, that hawthorn and purple lilac should not be juxtaposed in a garden – their colours fought against each other and should be separated by more regular shrubs to enhance the visual palette. Ceanothus with laburnum, again, another gardening sin despite the science of complementary colours – blue and yellow in such saturation was lacking in taste. Still, in the Old Rectory, they were too big to move now, and Dorothy had loved them.

Erica listened, noting that her mother's arrangements of plants in the garden was the reason why much of the original design had remained in tact for all these years.

Their circuit had ended in the driveway and their farewell did not leave Erica skittering back into the house for cover. She was pleasantly untroubled at being alone in the house – Harry had arranged for a couple of men to come and trim the trees and a man was being held for questioning by police for the attacks – two elements that provided a backdrop of security to spending time alone, meddling in the house.

She drifted into the kitchen and tried to arrange fallen horse chestnut blossoms into a vase. She placed them on the windowsill and eyed them closely, rows of finger nail-sized flowers, intricate as orchids, taking on an instantly shabby, withered appearance now shed from the tree. She considered the pyramids of snowy white lined with gold and red, disguised as regular creamy orbs until closely scrutinised. Her applied concentration, of being projected into the macro view of the world, was like a drift back into childhood, a release from the indelible cause and effect of the adult world.

The rattle of post through the letterbox brought Erica back to the task in hand. She collected the mail and trotted outside to retrieve the package from her car. The parcel was bound with broad layers of brown tape and was larger than its weight suggested. Beneath layers of bubble wrap Erica unearthed four white cardboard boxes with printed labels stuck on to them.

```
          Luteinil 500mg 200 caplets
   For administration only by a qualified
                  practitioner
```

"That's me." She said.

Erica spread the boxes on to the table and hovered at the stove, fiddling with a pot of percolating coffee. She poured herself a mug, spooned in a generous helping of sugar and inhaled the vapour for a few moments, looking back at the table. With a focus she normally reserved for the office, she worked through a number of simple tasks, sipping at her coffee and taking notes as she went along.

The first was to crush a single tablet with a pestle and mortar, sniff the white powder gently and then dab a little onto her tongue. It was odourless and tasted only a fraction as bitter as she had anticipated. She spat what she tasted into the sink and rinsed her mouth with water. Sipping from her coffee again she jotted in her notes that the sweetness in the coffee was the oral antidote to the sour taste of the chemical in her mouth.

After this she crushed a further ten tablets and weighed the powder using a set of tiny scales that had stood in the dresser for as long as she could remember. The weights were pieces of dark metal roughly carved into the shape of elephants. They had belonged to her mother and hence formed part of the clutter of the rectory that no one had dared suggest be thrown away. However, she had been dismayed when

Duncan had once commented that they were most likely to be scales for weighing hashish though Harry had refused to be drawn on the subject. Whatever their history, Erica was pleased that she had something with which to do the job at hand and carefully spooned the powder into measured quantities of water.

By ten o'clock she had attempted to dissolve one gram of the powder into various amounts of water to establish a saturation point and was setting out to test the effect of heat on the process. Gently raising the temperature of water using a pan over the hob and balancing a jam thermometer in it, she worked through a second set of tests to determine changes in solubility. She set down different glasses of resulting solutions to cool on the windowsill to see if the chemical precipitated out when the water cooled.

Placing the last glass onto the sill, she met a pair of pale brown eyes looking at her through the kitchen window.

Erica screamed and fell back into the table. Even though her brain had recognised in an instant who was confronting her through the glass, her instincts had ordered a yelp that was propelled into the steamy air.

"Sorry love!"

Erica raised a hand to gesture *no need to apologise* in response.

She propped herself up on the table and spoke out loud. "Why couldn't he knock like everybody else?"

She closed the kitchen door behind her and exited via the front entrance, keen to impart the message that the back door into the kitchen was out of bounds. Men had arrived to lop the trees, people that Erica had come to recognise over the years. They were pulling saws and ladders out of a rusting utility truck in order to undertake the pruning of the trees. Erica offered them coffee and disappeared inside again.

Within a couple of hours they had finished and Erica was tidying up in the kitchen. She had undertaken further tests to ascertain the effect of the dissolving process in different solvents – squash, apple juice and finally, beer. Her notes complete and the table cleared of the morning's activities she piled evenly weighed portions of crushed tablets collected in clear plastic sandwich bags into a box, covered them with a few old magazines, and had taken them upstairs to stow them under her bed. She burnt the empty white boxes in the grate in the lounge along with a few old bank statements so as to cover her tracks. Her actions were direct and effective; she had achieved her morning's objectives with minimum fuss and that was all there was to it.

Erica opened the door to the workmen when they had finished and collected their mugs from them.

"Bit early in the day to be drinking beer isn't it?"

Erica cocked her head and answered innocently. "Sorry?"

"I popped my head to in for a top up and saw you drinking beer." He laughed, forty years of smoking cigarettes rattling around in his lungs. "Taking after your dad then?" He laughed again and despite initially feeling irked at his prying, Erica detected no rudeness in his manner.

She smiled and leant casually on the door frame. "Yeah, just tasting some new stuff that dad's trying out." She reached into the hall to put the mugs on the shelf and returned to face him brightly. "So, how much do we owe you?"

"Oh, don't worry about that. Your dad'll settle up with us." He waved his arm dismissively and shuffled over to the truck.

"Fine, well thanks a lot then." Said Erica stepping inside the house, pleased that they were on their way.

"Yup. Cheerio love."

As far as Erica could tell, Harry's idea of 'settling up' with various tradesmen usually involved the exchange of beer for services. She was aware of a fairly generous annual allowance of beer bestowed upon the staff of the brewery but it was nothing equal to the amount required to pay for the upkeep of the Old Rectory. Erica had once raised this concern with Ellen who's view was simply that Harry's working class values were not necessarily honest ones. For as long as he was turning over a healthy profit for the owners, they were likely to turn a blind eye to any minor discrepancies in stock levels and he certainly considered himself to be above judgement on such matters.

She contemplated this err on the otherwise faultless view she held of her father from the doorstep as the workmen left. The truck pulled away stopping abruptly at the end of the driveway. The same man leant out of the window.

"They released Martin." He shouted.

Erica hesitated. "Who?" She asked.

"Martin Elliot. He was the one being held for questioning – Bill and Linda's son from the chip shop. Police couldn't charge him with anything – false accusation or something."

Erica held on to the side of the door with both hands, her head poking through a thin gap. "Oh right." She replied, in a voice that was virtually inaudible to him.

"Just thought you should know." He gestured towards the house. "Y'know. If there's no one else in now that we're off."

Erica didn't know what to say or how to act. The parameters within which she had afforded herself a decent night's sleep and a productive morning had suddenly changed. "Oh. Thanks. No, I'm fine. Dad'll be home soon." She said flatly, managing a weak smile.

"OK then. Cheerio."

The truck pulled away and Erica went inside. She plucked her handbag from the kitchen, her phone and keys and moved with the grace of a startled gazelle out of the front door and into her car.

SEVEN

A week later, Erica and Duncan were sitting outside a tapas bar in Barcelona. They had spent the day walking about Park Guell, eating ice cream, gazing out at the views and running their hands over Gaudi's undulating mosaic stone structures. It was day that had been peppered with minor disputes and bickering, but not misunderstandings so thorough as to cause a major row. The city had too much to offer for a weekend alone and Erica had been persuaded by Duncan to visit some of the places she had missed on a previous trip. The Sagrada Familia was therefore off the agenda and Park Guell was on, as were the various bars and exquisite restaurants of El Born.

It was early evening and sunlight hung in jagged strips along the tops of the stone walls and roofs. The street was relatively peaceful aside the occasional flurry of mopeds over the cobbles and car horns from the main street some blocks away. A couple of stray dogs were waved on by the bar staff and two smaller yapping dogs, chained to a lamppost, kicked up a fuss as they passed by.

The chime of a single church bell marked the hour and the arrival of a cool sea breeze making its way in land. It caused Erica to shiver and she pulled her cardigan over her shoulders in an effort to prolong the al fresco experience. She eyed a line of large, dried hams hanging inside behind the bar, frowned and looked back at Duncan. He was loudly tucking into a dish of king prawns and his knee was twitching furiously up and down. In most of Erica's attempts to wind down and take in the quiet luxuries of tourism, there was something about Duncan's behaviour which was able to take the edge off the moment. Currently there were two things: his leg movement and his method of eating prawns. The former reminded her of tendencies she had experienced as a child when it came to holding back a full bladder and simultaneously bolting a meal.

"Duncan, what *are* you doing?" She asked in a thin voice.

Duncan looked up and replied with his mouth full. "Enjoying the sumptuous delights of this splendid noshery." He smiled, reached for a cube of cheese from another dish and then moved back to the prawns.

"Quit the nimming." Said Erica, forcing a smile. "Please."

Duncan stopped moving his knee up and down and bit the head off a prawn. "Sorry." He said with his mouth full. A piece of prawn flesh flew from his lips and landed in a dish of potato wedges that sat in front of Erica.

"Jesus Duncan, that's disgusting. That's probably an eyeball or something."

Duncan chewed and swallowed audibly. "Eyeball, brain, oesophagus, it's all the same to me."

"Do prawns have –" Erica paused, not sure of the plural for 'oesophagus', "– *eating tracks* as such? I thought they were filter feeders."

"Dunno." Duncan — concentrating and unblinking — was still looking down and around at the spread of tapas on the table and reached for a slice of tortilla.

One of the stray dogs ambled up to their table and Erica reached down to scratch its head. It had short amber-coloured fur and large, pleading eyes. Erica looked furtively towards the bar, deftly plucked a slice of chorizo ham from the table and passed it to the dog.

"Ah little poochy." She muttered in soft baby voice. "Is that good? Is it? I bet it is. Would you like a prawn now little poochy? How about a little prawny munchy? Yum yum."

There was a smash from the bar as someone dropped a plate onto tiles and the dog made a hasty retreat into the road.

Duncan stared at Erica and then at the food on the table. "I don't understand you Erica." He said, agitated.

Erica looked up, pulled a 'please, not now Duncan' face and set to work on an oily dish of fried green beans and beef strips.

Duncan leant forward and spoke in a low voice, earnestly inquisitive. "How can you worship cats and dogs, claim to be an animal lover on the one hand, and on the other, eat cows and deer and god knows what else and wear leather shoes?"

Erica wiped her hands on her napkin, took a sip of beer and looked at Duncan evenly across the table. "I'm not arguing with you D." She said flatly. "When it comes to food, this is my choice."

Duncan returned her look and continued regardless. "Do you know what cows go through when they're slaughtered?" He asked.

Erica busied herself with bread and olives and said nothing.

Duncan continued sourly. "They're packed into trucks, cramped together, driven for miles, sometimes halfway across Europe, herded into slaughterhouses where they're terrified and can see and smell the death of the place, and then they're lined up and led one by one up some slimy ramp where a bolt's put through their head with varying degrees of accuracy, depending on the skill of the underpaid worker that happens to be on duty that day. They even pee themselves they're so scared." Duncan caught his breath. "It's wrong, it's unnecessary and what's more, we don't *need* meat. Can you imagine the outrage of we started doing that to dogs?" He concluded.

Erica answered quickly this time, leaning forward in imitation of Duncan's manner. "Ah, but you couldn't do it to dogs even if you tried. You could never get them to form an queue."

"What?"

"At the slaughterhouse. They'd never form an orderly line. Unless you used a poochy prod that is." Erica aimed the jab at her stone-faced boyfriend and waited.

"A what?" Duncan's face constricted with his question and he sat back. A couple at the next table burst into laughter and Erica waited for them to finish before she answered.

"A poochy prod. Rather like a cattle prod but for dogs." She fluttered her eyelashes and smiled, an attempt to inject some humour into the brew.

"For god's sake Erica, why do you always turn everything into a joke when you've been exposed for being a hypocrite?" Duncan scolded.

"If you've chosen abnegation as your path then that's up to you dearest." Erica's voice had dropped. She took a long slug of beer and sat back in her chair. "We're supposed to be on holiday Duncan, can we at least try acting like we are?"

"I don't consider that I'm denying myself any pleasure here Erica, on the contrary. My conscience is clear. Unlike yours." Duncan said in the voice of someone delivering a stern lecture. "I have been, and continue to be, baffled by how anyone in western society with half a brain and a reasonable grasp of science, can justify eating meat, and what's worse, think that domesticated house pets should in some way be treated differently."

"Duncan, you just ate a prawn." Said Erica, extending her words. "That's hardly what I would call a floating vegetable is it?"

They sat in silence for a while, drinking and looking about them, at the other folk sitting at tables and the passers by; anywhere but at each other. Eventually Erica reached across the table and took Duncan's hand.

"I hear you. OK? I don't eat lamb anymore, not since that holiday in Wales in the springtime, I buy free range meat when I'm at home and the last pair of trainers I bought were man-made. So c'mon love, live and let live eh?"

"Precisely my point Erica." Duncan pulled his hand away and looked down the street. He seemed to Erica to be concocting his own fury and she sat and waited for the next hit. He was clearly not in the mood for appeasing.

Duncan whipped his head back around to face Erica. "What is the matter with you anyway these days? Let's face it, something else is going on here. I don't understand why you've been so cool with me all spring it seems. I suspect it's all about the attacks or more likely, your mother's death and that it's upsetting you all these years on. Why are you carrying this enormous weight around with you at the moment? Either you've seriously gone off me or something's happened, something's triggered this mood. Whatever it is, I think I deserve an explanation. You should be moving closer to me, not further away."

Erica finished her glass of beer that she'd been swilling about, called the waiter over and ordered another one, which arrived promptly. Duncan remained silent, waiting for a response and picked at the edge of the table with his nail.

"I'm not going to argue with you D." She said quietly, allowing her hair to fall into her face. She took the beer glass in both hands and sighed. "I know sometimes I'm a bit harsh on you and I'm sorry." Her eyes flicked up to Duncan's momentarily. "But I know you and I think I can be myself with you." She paused again, contemplating weakly which version of an explanation would satisfy Duncan and wary that her own unravelling might begin if she started to explore the darker areas of her mind. She chose to stay on more solid territory.

"It's the house and everything in it. I live in this time capsule and it's beginning to drive me nuts. You know I found some of Jack's fur under the sofa when I was vacuuming the other day?" She didn't wait for a response. "Anyway, it's a fusty old shell of a place that is probably of more interest to a curator than to me these days and it's really beginning to get to me. I feel like I'm going mad. I mean, there's three bloody shotguns in the dining room. And when was the last time anyone actually dined in there?" She ran a hand through her hair and pulled hard at a knot with her fingers. "D'you know that row of wellies by the back door, well one of those pairs is mum's, complete with muddy soles from the last time she did the gardening. I've seen dad *dust* them for god's sake.

"I'm surrounded by a sea of clutter, of forced memories of mum imposed on me by this dear old man, who, on the surface looks perfectly normal but must surely have some issues locked away inside him. He should get out more, meet someone else. He's stuck in the past Duncan, I swear.

And the worst thing is, is that I learnt a long time ago to just shut it all out, pretend all mum's stuff isn't there, I mean, you know me – I don't *do* clutter – my bedroom is a shrine to minimalism." She looked up at Duncan.

"Indeed it is." He confirmed, nodding slowly.

"So now I feel bad that I just ignore it all, play dad's game of normality instead of really sitting down with him and asking him what's going on in his head, figuring out why he's stuck in the past. Even the veg we grow – most of the seeds are from things mum grew – sown, grown, harvested, resown, regrown, year after year. And the worst thing is –" She said, this time with a catch in her voice. "– Is that for the most part I can't really remember her all that well. Granted I had fifteen years with her but I was only really a child and I was the baby of the family. I mean, she was my mum and she was lovely, but she wasn't a friend, not like my sisters knew her. I envy them for that." She paused and Duncan opened his mouth to speak but Erica pressed on.

"You know, the things that I *do* remember about her are abstract and not connected in any way. I remember her playing the piano quite a bit and sitting next to her on the stool poking at the low notes but I don't know how old I was. I remember being scared when I broke her huge model ship that was her dad's and I cried my eyes out because I felt so bad but she sat beside me in bed and stroked my hair and said it was OK."

She took a breather, sipping urgently from her beer. At the release of a quiet burp, the corners of her mouth turned up a little.

"And I remember the time when for dinner, she served rhubarb tart with vegetables and me and Ellen finished it all without saying anything, and then for pudding we got rabbit pie and custard. She didn't know she'd mixed up the dishes from the freezer but Ellen and I couldn't stomach the rabbit and custard and when we told her she laughed so hard that she couldn't speak."

Duncan smiled. "But that's OK Erica. That's what memories are. No one has perfectly formed memories wrapped up in neat parcels in their mind that they can just switch on when they want to recall them. Memories are abstract – full stop – snippets of things, trivial or otherwise, randomly selected in our minds to stay put. I bet there's more in there that would come out if you talked to your sisters about your childhood. But thanks for explaining. I knew something was troubling you. I'm just glad it's not me." He sighed and leant forward. "And I didn't mean to take out my rage for the entire meat-eating populace on my girlfriend. Sorry."

Erica nodded noncommittally and slipped down a little in her chair.

"But I know what you mean." Said Duncan, resuming an upright posture. "It's the weirdest thing to be reminded of something you've not recalled since it happened. It's hard to establish what is stranger – somebody else reminding you of something for the first time in years or dealing with the frustration of knowing that there must be plenty more memories where they came from but that they are completely inaccessible to you without prompt." Duncan paused to take a sip of wine.

"One day, someone's going to produce a drug, some chemical that mimics the memory recollection process, and wham! – we'll be able to bring everything back – nothing we will have learnt will be wasted. Human wisdom would grow at the true rate it should according to age. Imagine the possibilities if you never forgot anything? We could be experts in anything we chose just so long as we did the reading. Although there'd be no one to work the supermarket checkout I suppose."

Duncan was looking into the middle distance, Erica irritated by the ease with which he could move between topics, in doing so, lose the seriousness of the subject under discussion – *her* subject. It was a habit that she had previously thought attractive in him but had recently found to be embarrassing when they were in company. At that moment though, she decided to go along with him and not claw the conversation back to herself as she had something to impart on the subject that was calculated to irk him.

"Actually you're wrong D. Some guy in Eastern Europe had some injury to his brain that meant he couldn't forget anything — I read it in a journal — he said it was awful, that his mind had become a scrap heap of information. He couldn't even forget the bath he had had last week, the countless journeys to and from work, each meal, everything, even moments of stillness. He said that his head had become full of junk and that it was unbearable. So in actual fact, we are programmed deliberately to forget things or we'd all go mad."

Erica's tone was flat, a deliberate attempt to avoid sounding like she was delivering a lecture.

Duncan returned a weak smile and answered gently. "Whatever Erica, whatever. But you're off the point. The point is, you're not the first person to lose a parent."

"*I'm* off the point?"

Duncan ignored her. "I don't carry the weight of the world on my shoulders with me as an adult and I certainly don't take out my problems with it all on you."

"Yes, but you were only f—"

"It doesn't matter – five, fifteen, I was a child too. I have memories of dad and if anything, am driven even more insane than you could ever imagine by having to clutch at what little my brain is able to offer me in terms of images that I can recall." He stopped to catch his breath. "But my mum and I are close and in some ways that's a small compensation. In fact, I doubt mum and I would be able to talk so freely with each other if it wasn't for the fact that there was only the two of us for so many years."

"Said Duncan, wearing the latest in rose-tinted spectacles." Was Erica's trite response. She was finally and irreconcilably, riled by him.

Duncan stared into Erica's eyes with a fierceness that told her she'd stepped over a line.

Erica was swift to continue. "I just mean that you left home pretty sharpish and moved south. When was the last time you went to Scotland? Nine months ago? It was before Christmas."

"It was November actually. And no I haven't seen her for a while but the Polish community in Glasgow are her family now. Mum and I talk on the phone every week and I'd put money on me and her having some rather more realistic conversations over the phone than you ever have with Harry."

Duncan had raised his voice and Erica strained to hear the language that their fellow diners were using in order to establish whether they would have understood their argument. She looked at Duncan's chubby round face and around at the half-eaten dishes on the table.

"Sorry." She said again in a whisper and yet thinking *why am I reproaching myself?*

"Stop apologising Erica, it's becoming shallow and meaningless. Do whatever it is you need to do – move out of the house, get another job, end this relationship, but for god's sake stop being such a bitch to me."

"Duncan!" Erica hissed, rolling her eyes towards the other diners.

"I mean it. You don't treat anyone else so casually and you certainly never used to speak to me like this. Something's got to give."

"OK, OK." Said Erica, hushing him. "What *has* got in to you?"

Ignoring her, Duncan went on, carelessly spitting his words. "Has it ever occurred to you that the only reason that your dad still lives in that house and harbours all that stuff is because he thinks it keeps *you* happy?"

A bolt of lightning whipped across the sky and thunder smacked in angry waves around the old buildings. A number of the diners jumped, including Erica who knocked her glass over. She dabbed urgently at spilt beer with her napkin between the dishes of food and caught a quiet sigh of exasperation from Duncan as he went inside to pay. Erica stood up in preparation to depart and looked up at the sky through a gap in the buildings towards the coast. There was no clearly defined bank of cloud over the sea marking the front line of the storm, instead, a seamless gradation of dark blue to orangey grey, like a roughly washed watercolour. Erica eyed the patches of deepest grey, wary for the next strike and felt the first spits of rain on her skin.

Duncan returned promptly and propelled her into the street in the direction of their hotel, his hand pressed into the small of her back like a parent marching a badly behaved child.

Their short journey was punctuated by bursts of torrential rain that saw Erica and Duncan pinned to doorways, Erica wincing, her eyes closed and her head buried in Duncan's chest who stood resolutely with his hands by his sides.

The bar of the three-star Pomodora Hotel was in the basement. It was dimly lit and poorly maintained but hosted a jolly proprietor and a group of middle-aged men who were keenly following the progress of FC Barcelona on a high wall-mounted television. Erica had gone there immediately they had arrived back and Duncan had followed on after collecting their room key. She ordered two shots of tequila with salt and lemon and a bottle of red wine.

The tension between the couple was relieved by the quick slip into intoxication that was afforded by the tequila and they spoke formally in short sentences about their plans for the following morning, what sightseeing they could fit in before departing for the airport and what had stirred them most from the day's venture to Park Guell. They were relieved to be out of the storm and their own accompanying disagreements.

Duncan began rambling in less stilted tones about previous visits to the city and Erica looked at him, not hearing his words. She decided that a sudden moment of objective consideration that came upon her during his rant was in fact an epiphany of sorts: this man was a friend and a friend only. If she could not compromise for his mannerisms and his fury at her eating preferences, then he was surely not a life partner in the making. Take away the fact that they were in a relationship and these traits became a faint blemish on an otherwise solid friendship. He was dependable, intelligent and honest and to someone somewhere, would make the good father to a brood of children.

And there it was.

She had half a mind that Duncan was thinking the same thing and held his hand as he talked, overcome with the melancholy of someone poised to deliver unwelcome news and considering for herself, an altered future. If the spate of crime in Brenly continued and if the police found no immediate resolution, she could ask Harry to hold off on business trips for a while or spend more time at Janice's. It was a request that should not necessitate an explanation especially if she was to return with news of the split from her boyfriend.

When the football match was finished she suggested that they have an early night in order to make the best of their final day. They bade brief farewells in broken Spanish to the few remaining men in the bar and headed up to their room. Duncan made immediately for the bathroom clutching his toothbrush but Erica blocked his path. She made short work of making her intentions clear to him and he relaxed into her attentions without hesitation. If this was to be the last night she would share a bed with him then she intended to relieve her guilt for the news she was to deliver the following day.

After a brief fumble with clothes and bedside lamps, Duncan was naked and without his glasses, and appeared to Erica to be even more vulnerable a creature than when she first met him, someone to be mentored or propped up in some way, someone that was easy to lead. She watched his face as she moved over him, observing how he closed his eyes and how this, and his astutely traditional approach to sex, was another of his features that held little appeal to her. She leant forward and allowed her hair to drop forward and onto his face, playing with her thick dark curls that now moved back and forth over the taught skin of his forehead. She saw her hair as a toupé covering his baldness and smiled as she arranged it at different angles between the two strips of cropped hair that remained over his ears. It was an activity that kept her both amused and distracted.

When Duncan signalled by a deep gasp that he wanted Erica to stop, he opened his eyes and saw her smiling back at him, focusing her attention on his forehead, her face a picture of complete absence from the moment.

"Are you OK…?" He asked, quietly, breathless.

"Yes I'm fine."

She sat up, patted his loose belly in a matter of fact way which bounded back in broad waves, and made a slow exit to the bathroom.

EIGHT

The sky was an impenetrable tarmac grey and the air was made damp by days of sheeting rain. Harry made a run for the brewery in a downpour that had flooded the yard. He bounded up the iron stairs two at a time and burst into the offices panting and with water running down his face. His feet were sopping wet in his shoes and he stood dripping in the small reception area blatantly seeking sympathy. He was vaguely disappointed that he had an audience of one – the marketing director, Izzie.

"Good lord." He said, feebly shaking his arms.

Izzie moved slowly from her desk into the kitchen and returned with a couple of hand towels.

"I was watching you on the camera. Why didn't you wait in the car 'til it had calmed down?" She asked. "Here you go." She handed him the towels and shook her head as if gently scalding a child.

Harry took the towels and roughly rubbed his hair in a way made possible by the fact that it was never styled as such. He slid his feet out of his shoes and peeled off his socks. "Look." He said, holding them up.

"Eddie's in with a client!" She hissed pointing behind her to another of the offices.

"Oh." He put his hand up to his mouth in exclamation and with it, a wet sock. He grinned and tiptoed animatedly past her and into his office. He immediately put his head back round the door.

"You haven't got any spare –"

"Socks? No." Said Izzie. "There's wellies downstairs though. Not sure they'll go with that suit mind. But anyway, where have you been?" She didn't wait for an answer. "I've got messages for you." She paused, expecting Harry to offer an acknowledgement but heard only the sound of drawers being opened and closed.   "Frank called. Said could you give him a ring at some point. He's put the car in the drive and the keys through the letterbox but no hurry to settle up." Again Harry said nothing and Izzie moved into the doorway of his office to face him. "Someone called Anita called but didn't want to leave a message." Izzie raised an eyebrow but Harry continued to search through a filing cabinet, pulling out a crumpled t-shirt and tennis shorts. "And Ellen. Said could you call her at work." Izzie concluded, her arms folded, watching Harry assess the dry clothes he had found.

He looked up and absentmindedly put the clothes on top of a pile of papers on his desk. "Right-o. Thanks." He said and picked up the phone. Before dialling any numbers he turned again to his colleague. "Anything else?" It was said through a warm smile but Izzie took the cue to leave him alone.

Harry caught Ellen at her desk at work and started the conversation by saying that it was good to hear from her and was it raining as hard in London.

Ellen was prompt in her replies and cut to the chase. "Janice has been on at me again about the house dad. She wants her share of the inheritance sooner rather than later because she's thinking of putting the boys through school in September."

Harry offered no acknowledgement so she continued. "She wants them to go to private school and needs the cash. Obviously. I don't think even Keith can stretch to that, what with their mortgage."

"Clearly." Said Harry, his good mood extinguished in an instant. "And what's wrong with good old state education? You didn't fare so badly did you?"

Ellen replied, her voice tired and impatient, as if the conversation had already gone on long enough and she had better things to be getting on with. "Look, I can't speak for Janice, I'm just giving you a bit of warning as the subject is going to come up again. And to be fair, I don't think mum would have objected to it in the grand scheme of things, do you?"

Harry fiddled with the phone cord and Ellen pressed on. "And well, it's been ten years and you did say you wanted us to hang on for Erica's sake." She paused. "Which we have done."

"Yes I know, I know. But I don't think that now is the right time, not with Erica being the way she is at the moment." Harry was standing up and staring at his pale toes protruding from the trouser legs of his suit.

"What way? What do you mean?"

"She split up with Duncan when she got back from that weekend in Barcelona, and she's very low. I think she needs a bit more time to figure things out. Selling the house would just upset her too much."

"She split up with Duncan?"

Ellen's voice was raised and Harry did a poor job of hiding his delight that Erica had confided in him before her sisters.

"Yes, didn't she tell you?" He asked.

Ellen sighed. "Less of the rhetoric dad. Evidently not."

Harry continued. "So I was rather hoping she'd have settled down by now then I'd feel a lot happier about us both moving out."

"Right. So you're telling me that we're going to have to wait until Erica goes up the aisle before you'll put the Old Rectory on the market?"

"Uhm... Well, not exactly. I hadn't thought of it quite like that." Harry wiggled his toes again, straining to see how long his nails were.

"Great, nice one dad. Well have fun explaining that to Janice. I've got to go."

"No. Hang on love." Harry spoke pleadingly, regretting having handled the news of Erica's split with Duncan so poorly.

But Ellen didn't give him a chance and hung up. Harry sat down heavily in his chair resting his elbows on the desk. He sighed and rubbed his forehead.

On cue, Izzie walked in and handed him a pair of white sports socks.

"Here you go." She said brightly, and then "Everything OK?"

"Perfectly fine, thank you." Was Harry's terse reply.

"It's Erica's birthday soon isn't it? I seem to remember some last minute shopping on your part same time last year."

Harry swivelled to face Izzie, his head still in his hands. She remained still.

"Make a big fuss of her on her birthday." She offered. "A good old family gathering. You were all apart for Christmas and Easter."

"What?" Harry looked at her full in the face, frowning.

"Erica. Make a big deal of her birthday. Have a cake and some people over, y'know. Get her something really special or take her shopping or something. It's next month isn't it?"

Harry, irked by Izzie's blatant invasion of his privacy refused the offer of the socks, muttered something about a delivery and ushered her out of his office. He closed the door and let the idea wash over him, considering that on this occasion, she might actually be right.

Erica stood at the bus top, her head pushed up as far as possible inside her umbrella, content that the broken metal spokes in her immediate line of vision were the current focus of her attention. The rain drummed against the black plastic skin in irregular pulses according to the shift of the wind. Waves of puddle water kicked up by the traffic caught the edge of her boots. It was October in June and was the subject on everyone's lips engaged in trivial conversation in the corridors of offices and at shop counters the country over.

Third back in the line she felt no anguish for the expected bus, just an acceptance that there would inevitably be a protracted wait given the heavy rain and full streets of traffic. She thought of Duncan and how their brief meeting in the refectory that day had rendered them both awkward and unsure of each other. A vision of Connor flicked into her mind's eye but was drowned out by a curious mix of guilt and quashed expectations. She thought randomly of Harry, the car, the umbrella, her finances, Carmi, her sisters; tired thoughts at the end of a long day.

Whilst her car was being repaired, she had enjoyed the extension of her work routine in commuting into the city by bus and living out of a bag. It had suited her mood to take her pace down a gear and sit anonymously twice a day on hard nylon-covered seats, her cheek pressed against the steamy glass. She had even taken to a preference of seat on the bus – second from back, lower deck – from which to observe the comings and goings of other passengers and to note also, other regulars who sat in their own preferred place. By the end of the week she was on nodding terms with two others – one uncomfortably pregnant girl in her early twenties and a wiry suited woman nearing retirement. Erica thought that they were on the verge of conversation that morning when the bus had been particularly late and everyone's silent sympathies had been for the pregnant girl standing patiently in an ill-fitting summer jacket. But they did not break into speech. The rain had kept pace with Erica's mood and her morbid introspection stood no chance of relief without a break in the weather; she was in no mood for idle chat.

The buildings of the city were awash with Cotswold's finest: limestone lining twisting lanes and quirky crooked crevices. The only souls to remain aesthetically untouched by its architecturally alluring irregularity were those who focused only on the residues of pollution, tidemarks of filth from a thousand buses a day. Many of them were born in to the city, immune to its beauty, dwelling only on its qualities as a centre for employment: people moved in and out in a voiceless mass at day break and day end, the homeless sought refuge in back street community halls and the pollution made claim to a rise in asthma in the city's children.

For the time being, Erica was in this group, keeping her head down and turning a blind eye to growing accumulations of coordinated tourists. Despite her privileged status as an employee of the university, she allowed her capricious nature to dwell on the more sullen elements of her life as it stood. There would be no summer to speak of — it was England after all — and long-term plans were temporarily off the agenda. She had spent two nights at Carmi's while her husband was away and had allowed Janice to pluck her from the bus stop one evening and drive her out to the parochial isolation of the cottage to dine with her nephews. Janice had been swift in action following the alert from Ellen that Erica was at a low ebb, but had not pried. Erica had offered little by way of explanation, muttering briefly over the washing up that it was all over with Duncan, that she had made a mistake.

The absence of the expected euphoria in breaking from Duncan – the romantic notion that she would feel like a caged bird set free – was a revelation to Erica. The feelings she had nurtured for him over the three years they had been together, the habits and nuances of their interplay, had become ingrained in her. She did not foresee that the split would be a dampener to her momentum for addressing the disquiet in her mind and so she retained an emotional stasis over the weeks following the weekend in Barcelona.

Professor Singh had twice encouraged her to take lunch with her and Erica had accepted the invitations awkwardly. The second time, she had driven them both to a remote pub on the Thames and in-between short outbursts regarding the strategic direction of the department, had tried to impart nuggets of personal advice that seemed contrived in their deliverance.

Erica had failed, in her own view, to engage at a level that was being sought and thought her boss's motives to be transparent. Anita's pragmatic approach to Erica's distress was baffling.

In dwelling on the year's events, Erica had surprised herself with the clarity and focus with which she had coolly released Duncan from her life and struggled to understand how she could have been cruel to him. She had attempted to allay her own personal dislike of herself and of what she perceived to be her heartless calculation of events: she was overly attentive to Carmi's problems, she posted cheques to charitable organisations and signed up to a full weekend in August looking after her nephews. She was, as Harry kept reminding her, *putting a brave face on.*

Erica felt her phone vibrate from within her bag but chose to ignore it. The queue was making a concerted shuffle nearer to the kerb, a sure sign that someone had spotted the bus and it was too much to be grappling with an umbrella, a bus pass and a phone in the rain. The bus pulled in slowly, tormenting the people in the queue further; Erica sprung aboard and took her seat. She pulled her phone out of her bag to see the number of the missed call. It was Harry.

Erica checked the message he had left and made a conscious decision not to call him back. He had asked her if she wanted to have Janice, the kids and Ellen over for her birthday and she frowned as she listened thinking that was probably the last thing she would like to do on her birthday next month. She hurriedly sent a text to Carmi asking her to keep the evening of her birthday free, keen to secure a plan that would keep her out of the house.

Carmi called back immediately.

"Hey you – where are you?" Carmi asked.

"I'm on the bus, being one of those annoying people that talks on their phone." Erica smiled and rested her head against the heavily condensated window.

"Of course I'll come out on your birthday, dipsy. Goes without saying."

"Oh lovely, thanks. I needed to secure your presence before dad tries to pin me down to some agonising family get-together."

"Ah, I see. Well he'll do it anyway if he really wants to. Just because you're busy on your birthday doesn't mean he can't work round it."

Erica contemplated the simplicity of this truth for a second but Carmi interrupted her thoughts. "I'm just heading off to a step class at the gym and I wondered if you fancied joining me. I've got a guest pass and some spare kit. We could get a take out afterwards."

"Yeah, why not? I'll get off at the ring road."

"Excellent. Sorry, I should have asked earlier then you could have come back with me after work."

Everyone was on to Erica, everyone that knew and loved her, only Carmi was perhaps the most subtle and most effective in her action to draw Erica away from her navel gazing. Whilst no one could expect her to be seriously heartbroken for any length of time, her family's attempts to console her were, in Erica's view, contrived and over sensitised. There were times when she enjoyed being the baby of the family for all the attention she garnered, but right now she wanted to be the adolescent again — moody and spontaneous — which was why Carmi's approach appealed to her.

Within half an hour, they were standing in the pristine aerobics studio of Shakers Sports Centre, surrounded on three sides by floor-to-ceiling mirrors and on another, by windows overlooking the indoor pool. Erica was standing in front of a step platform in baggy lycra and a pair of aged black plimsolls. Carmi was a full four sizes larger than Erica and appeared to her to be someone that pursued fitness classes doggedly to little effect on the width of her backside — her intended target. Carmi was almost too fit, built heavily with broad, muscular shoulders and a wide flat stomach. In Eric's view, she should have climbed mountains, trekked the Great Wall of China, cycled and sailed around the world but had instead been born within two streets of her current house and had left the country only twice in her life. A waste of an outgoing personality and a body that could have built bridges.

Erica was at the front of the class and could see Carmi limbering up behind her, reflected in the mirror. The instructor, an ample redhead called Toni, sporting hot pants and a vest, and a microphone hooked over her ear, called them into line and switched on a small boombox.

Toni had a different rhythm to the one echoing from the stereo, which made following sets of movements difficult and predicting her next move, impossible. There were only six other girls in a studio that could have held at least thirty, all grimacing and panting along with their leader.

After the warm up was over, Toni dished out hand weights and proceeded to yell "Pump it girls! Pump!" as she demonstrated raising the weights up and down from shoulder height. After a few minutes of this, she increased the speed of the music being played by crudely turning a knob on the stereo. It was the musical equivalent of turning Donna Summer into Pinky and Perky.

Erica smiled at Carmi conspiratorially who looked down, hiding her own amusement at the crass increase in tempo. As the class attempted to keep up, Erica fought to move her arms up and down at the required intervals and moved her focus away from the instructor to her own reflection. She watched herself, this leggy bird in oversized leggings, her knees knocking as she stepped and her feet entirely out of synch with her arms. She felt the first tinges of hysteria rise up from her torso to her face. She was out of time, out of step, her face contorted with the effort of lifting the weights and stepping to the over-paced music. Another minute later and she burst out laughing, dropping both weights on to the floor. Her foot caught the lip of the step and she fell backwards in a relaxed roll, her hysterics so far advanced that no sound came from her open mouth.

Carmi, though ultimately embarrassed, put her weights down, helped Erica to her feet and escorted her out of the room mouthing an apology to Toni who stood perplexed at the front of the class.

"Is she OK?" She asked bleakly into the microphone. The other girls carried on stepping and lifting, well practised and as if in support of their instructor, ignoring the flagrant exhibitionism of their departed co-stepper.

Carmi stood outside the studio in a corner of the sports complex, her hands on her hips looking her friend up and down. Erica was bent double, laughing, trying to speak but unable to produce a coherent sentence.

"Well look at you." Carmi said, smiling, a giggle catching her own voice. "Look at *you*."

Within a fortnight, the rain had ceased and in its wake were long days of sunshine broken by spells of intense humidity and storms. It brought lawnmowers out of hibernation and compelled the midsummer blooms to emerge from the wet spring. The rapeseed had long since turned and the cabbagey smell of the ripening seeds wafted into Brenly from the surrounding farmland.

The once frenetic talk of the crimes in the area was now reduced to passing comments between neighbours over garden fences and with it, easier nights sleep and a slide into less vigilant home security routines. The consensus in the post office queue and at the counter in the Coop was that the heavy police presence had frightened the perpetrator away; the older folk quick to establish that there hadn't been such community spirit in the village since the Second World War.

Erica caught this wave of optimism and coupled with the change in the weather, brought herself back to the point of focus she had engaged with a month previous. She had taken to escaping to the garden after work in the hot spells to drink a glass of wine before Harry got home.

The Old Rectory stood in a two-acre site, the even-sided house sitting directly in the centre of the square plot. Aside the well-tended driveway and entrance, the other parts of the garden were clearly divided as kempt and unkempt. Around the back of the house stood the large shabby greenhouse busting with vegetables and a vine that had rooted through the bottom of its pot and woven its way up and out of the rusting iron frame. Harry enjoyed the idea that it was more of a Victorian glasshouse than simply a common-or-garden greenhouse, which was his main reason for doggedly repairing it year on year rather than replacing it with something altogether more solid.

Amid the variously tended patches of rough grass around the greenhouse were pristine oblongs of earth, home to neat teepees of sweet peas and runner beans, rows of lettuces, carrots and broad beans. A couple of neglected chicken runs that remained by the rear perimeter and a large rhubarb patch marked the edge of what was the garden and what was officially wild with nettles, holly bushes and ivy. Mature oak, poplar and horse chestnut were dotted around the perimeter and had turned a long wall at the front of the garden into an undulating length of leaning stone by the rise and push of their hefty roots. The old chicken house served as the potting shed, mended over the years by panels from an old conservatory and off-cuts of felt that Harry had come by. A ditch of about four feet deep lined the perimeter of the plot to the sides and rear — a moat of sorts that would have once kept the heathens from the door.

Beyond the moat were narrow fields, kept safe by the parish council from property developers but otherwise left to go wild, prime for grazing with lush grasses, but not touched by domestic stock, just a place for early morning dog walkers, foxes, field mice and shrews. The whole thing was a slice of wilderness, cut off from the wider expanses of wood and farmland that surrounded Brenly. It rendered the dawn chorus alive with rare songs and the ready call of collared doves and wood pigeons.

Erica's favourite spot was on the south facing side of the house near the back door where she had a clear view of the driveway and the fields. The luxury and privilege that growing up in the Old Rectory had given her had passed her by in her youth and whilst she was acutely aware that ninety five per cent of her friends had long since left home, she remained wrapt by the house at times, oscillating between her pull to leave and find a different kind of independence that she had explained to Duncan, and the fear that leaving might in some way be the catalyst for losing it altogether. Now was one of those moments when the simple pleasures of the garden on a midsummer's evening leant nothing to the argument for moving out.

She sat in an uncomfortable iron chair and drank wine from an elegant plastic glass, absently rolling the stem between her thumb and forefinger. She observed the newly-mown lawn near the front of the house and the sunflowers recovered again from the heat of the day. A tangle of purple-flowering clematis that climbed the south wall of the house drew bees in abundance and the neighbourhood was quiet save for the odd rumble of a passing car and the peak and cluck of summer bird song. The satisfaction of sitting in the garden washed over her giving its own unique fulfilment. She considered it for what it was: the same rush as watching red kites make circles in a Chiltern valley or walking down the soft path of a chestnut avenue drinking the perfume of bluebells and wild garlic. The garden though, was nature in unnatural formations, sections of it were weedless and packed with competing fare. It gave it that extra edge that the view of a valley could never incite – that desire to pluck and pick, tie-up and tame and make just-so.

Erica remembered as a child being allocated a small plot at the back of the house in which she chose to grow marigolds in neat rows. They had sat in the ground, a garish distraction from the vegetables that surrounded them, but were steadily annihilated by slugs and snails. Dorothy had been dismissive as to their fate, repelled by bedding plants in general, and Erica considered that it was Harry that seemed to have the most time for her in the garden despite their difficult start in life. Dorothy seemed to always be in a hurry there, hacking at the rhubarb or thrusting colanders at her daughters and sending them out to pick blackcurrants and raspberries. But Harry would take her for rides in the wheelbarrow and rake up the autumn leaves into huge mounds. Erica would throw herself into them and wriggle about screeching playfully until a bug frightened her out or her sisters piled in after her. Then when the lawn was cleared of detritus, it was Janice who got to light the bonfires of dried up bracken and leaves – she was stable and mature beyond her years even before she hit puberty.

It was moving into more diverse circles at university and through various Saturday jobs in greengrocers and nursing homes, that Erica first begun to realise what a fortunate and privileged childhood she had had. Losing her mother at the time in her life when she was moving from this flowery chaos into womanhood was the icy hand of reality freezing her youthful optimism in one swift blow. The shock of it all made future recollections of the days around Dorothy's death difficult to muster: they were dimly lit shadowy memories of muffled voices behind closed doors and sitting between her sisters in hospital corridors.

Erica shuddered. When her thoughts had begun to destabilise her in the past, she'd reached for Duncan, sometimes Ellen and Janice and sometimes Carmi. She thought she missed Duncan, the freedom of calling him up at any time, sharing ideas of no consequence, knowing that he was there. Did she miss him or did she miss the thing that he represented – an appendage to her life, the all-knowing friend?

She picked up her phone from the table and fiddled with the buttons, scrolling down to his number, her thumb hovering over the *call* button. She scrolled away from it and selected *Connor Fairchild* from her list of numbers instead. Erica looked up and out onto the fields and the driveway, searching vacantly for a minute, then returned to the phone.

"Oh my god."

She sat up straight in the chair, pressed the *call* button and put the phone to her ear. The number rang out and connected her to an answering service that mechanically read back the number she had dialled.

"Oh hi, Connor, uh, it's me, Erica Ford. We met at the presentation you gave in Brenly at the end of April, oh and yes of course, you came round here that time afterwards so yes, well, that's me. I'm not sure if you remember." Erica paused and rested her forehead in her free hand and bit her lip. "Well, um, it's been a while but I've been busy and I was just still wondering you were OK to meet up or talk or something sometime soon about the thing I was talking about – my research – and if it was OK if I could ask you some questions or maybe someone else you could point me in the direction of." She was speaking quickly and had lost track of what she had already said. "So, if you could give me a call that would be great, but if not, that's also fine. OK, um, thanks, yeah. Bye." Pause. "Oh, it's Erica Ford by the way, yeah sorry. Did I already mention that?" The mechanical voice cut in to announce that her message time had ended.

"Damn!" She put the phone back on the table with a heavy clack.

A wood pigeon made an ungainly flight from the roof of the house to the patio and marched around her in quick circles, blinking and pecking at the ground. The church bell chimed seven o'clock and Erica was reminded that Harry would be home soon. She finished her drink and headed inside to fetch some bread for the bird, muttering under her breath – "oh my god, oh my god" – as she padded back and forth.

NINE

Often, when the boys were safely despatched at the school gates, Janice would drive into town and enjoy a large cappuccino and chocolate chip muffin in the bookstore. She would grab a couple of new titles from the science section and settle down to flick through the introductions and to take in the main tenet of the books for future regurgitation among friends. She never bought any as such, her only purchases being trashy celebrity magazines or any of the music titles that were offering a free CD that month. It was these excursions into fact gathering that she considered were keeping her brain alive in the otherwise mind-numbing possibilities offered by full-time childcare.

After five years in Bristol studying medicine, and a further three working towards becoming a paediatrician, she had married Keith, a hospital manager ten years her senior – complete with teenage daughter. Within a year she had had the twins and had given up work to look after them. By all accounts her career was barely off the ground before she was removed from it to care for the boys and forge a decent relationship with her new stepdaughter. She had attempted some freelance work as an editor for a low-key medical publisher, but had found herself dozing over dry texts when she was able to give any time to it. Most of her former work colleagues and friends from university were well into their careers. Janice had endeavoured to keep up with them on a social footing but had found it hard to relate the joy of bringing twins into the world to friends whose motivations at the time were driven solely by professional success.

She was a serious person by nature that tended to a predilection for harbouring grudges and sometimes, archaic disciplining of the children. Keith had congratulated her on licking Cleo into shape but had more than once reminded her to "just chill out" when it came to the strict schedule she set for the boys. He had also questioned why she bothered to cling to such a dry set of friends when the circles he mixed in – at the hospital and through the cricket club – were far more adept at a knees-up. Janice herself wasn't sure either. She had been quiet and academic at school, unsure of where she would find her niche in life. She had struggled at university and sat many retakes to obtain the status she had craved. Being a homemaker though had felt altogether more comfortable. She had excelled at the challenge presented by taming a once unwieldy Cleo, a talent she had nurtured when Erica herself was motherless and adolescent. She had unsuccessfully fought Harry in private to allow Erica to move in with her after she had graduated, and had taken to being the matriarch of her own and other's broods with aplomb. Ellen was the only one that was slightly out of reach from her motherly domain but they were close nonetheless.

She had wanted more children after the twins and Keith had been amenable to the idea, but none came. He had rejected her requests for pursuing the matter medically saying that "What will be, will be," and "Why worry, we've already got three?". His interest in his wife was regular and unbending but not exceptionally romantic though his interest in his children grew as they grew. Cleo had severely criticised him on occasion for being interested in his flock only if they could fit in with his hobbies and not the other way around; Janice, in her silence, had not come to Keith's defence. The twins were boys and would, god willing, have an interest in cycling and cricket as he did, or they were all doomed. They led a comfortable life in a four-bedroom cottage with an allowance from Keith that came without grudge. It had been an entirely satisfactory lifestyle. Until recently.

Janice stood outside the bookstore and looked through the glass at the summer reading titles and two-for-one bargains. The streets were clogged with tourists that jostled among the city folk in ambling packs. She could feel the sun irritating her skin on her bare arms and was agitated by its intensity so early on in the day. Janice had three hours to kill before collecting the boys but her usual enthusiasm for her morning's indulgence in the back room of the shop had been extinguished by other thoughts. She had been dwelling on the fact that the boys would start school full-time in September and what impact that would make on her justification for remaining at home. The boys were at a decent state school and they were doing well.

She was unsettled by Keith's desire to stay where he was on the career ladder, him hinting lately that two salaries over one would allow them decent holidays and a secure future. Janice wanted the sale of the Old Rectory to stave off her inevitable return to work more than she desired the boys to attend a private school, but she had no intention of sharing that with him, or with anyone in the family. Erica would cope with the change – she was twenty-six next month and should have moved out by now anyway. It would do her good to get away from the old place – she'd always have a roof over her head at the cottage if she needed it. Janice would make sure of that.

She turned her back to the shop, leant against the glass and dialled Harry's number from her mobile.

Harry's voice was distant, exuding a reluctant acceptance of what was to follow. He remarked that it had been well over a month since he'd seen his grandchildren.

"I'll bring them over to the brewery in the holidays. Anyway that's not why I was calling."

Harry was silent.

"I was wondering if we might have a chat about our inheritance from mum i.e. if you were thinking of selling the Old Rectory."

Again, Harry remained silent. Janice, aware of the strain she was putting on him, continued.

"It's been ten years dad." She paused. "Dad?"

"Yes, I'm here."

"Can you talk or should I call back later?" Janice was matter of fact.

"No, no. You carry on." Harry's voice was low, sighing through his words.

"We've held off – me and Ellen – for a while as you requested and to be honest, if it wasn't for Auntie Dot insisting on it, then I'd probably have brought this up earlier."

"Yes, I'm aware of that."

"Well? What are your plans? If you gave Erica her share, then she could buy somewhere herself, get some independence. And anyway, I'd like to send the boys to private school and we can't do that presently, not on Keith's salary." Janice bit her lip, waiting for Harry to comment on the possibilities of her taking paid employment to fund his grandsons' private education.

He didn't rise to it. "So?"

"Janice have you no attachment to the stunning and incredible house in which you were raised? Has the privilege that was bestowed on you to spend your childhood in such a place completely passed you by?"

Janice shifted her weight onto one foot. "No dad, it hasn't passed me by."

Harry kept pace. "Have you no desire to keep the old place in the family, to allow your sons to spend time there, maybe even inherit it themselves one day? What is it that you want me to do – buy you out or something? You know I couldn't afford to do that."

"Dad, you're Head of Brewing, or whatever it is you call yourself these days, you've got no mortgage – of course you can bloody well afford to buy me out and no I don't care if Casper and Ben don't spend any time there – I never expected them to. In case you've forgotten, I don't have the kinds of memories of the old place that I think you'd like me to." Janice had raised her voice and was staring out through the crowds on the street, her eyes unfocused.

She continued. "And anyway, mum was never that attached to the place, she spent half her time complaining about having to keep it clean and tidy when her main interest was in making sure we were happy. I doubt if she was here today that she'd be clinging to it like you are. She'd have found somewhere much smaller to live in I'm sure."

"I doubt that very much actually. She fought me tooth and nail to stay there when we were skint, when you were a nipper. It was all she had left of her parents." Harry let his words hang. "And what would you know about what mum would and wouldn't want if she were alive today eh?" Janice heard the sound of Harry's office door slamming – he was on his feet and he was pacing about.

"I could well ask you the same question Harry." Janice spat her words into her phone.

"A lot more than you give me credit for young lady. But if you want me to buy you out, then fine, I'll look into it, but I'm not selling Erica's home just because it suits you."

"Fine."

"I'll need to talk to her about all this. I don't want her thinking she can't have her share too or equally that she has to move out because you want yours." Harry was quieter. "Just give me some time and I'll get back to you."

"Oh, here we go. You need more time. What a surprise." Janice's palms were moist and she looked about her, aware of her own presence as a woman speaking loudly into a phone in the street.

"I'll get back to you soon, don't worry. "Said Harry reluctantly. "But there's something I'd like you to do for me. Could you please come over around Erica's birthday next month for dinner – all of you – Cleo and the boys, Ellen too obviously. Maybe on the Sunday so the boys can have a play about here. Erica needs cheering up and it would be good to get us all together."

Janice pulled herself away from the window and stood up straight. "You are unreal. How could that possibly be good? I'll come, OK, fine. I doubt Cleo will want to but I'll ask her anyway. But get a grip on this dad – when was the last time we all sat down for a meal together and when has it ever been good? And are you sure Erica wants this? She knows you and I have issues."

"Well perhaps that's what I'm driving at. We could all be on best behaviour for her sake."

"Good lord. I'm not pretending anything for you."

"I know. But you could do it for your little sister."

Janice was defeated and exhausted. She bade her father a terse farewell saying that she'd speak to Ellen about the meal. Heading into the street with no clear destination in mind, tears fell from her eyes in thick streams and she pushed her sunglasses up her nose to catch them.

At that moment, Connor Fairchild was padding about his flat, stereo on, singing along to the music. He set a mug down on a low coffee table, sat heavily into the sofa and leant forward to activate his laptop that was perched on the table. He was dressed in jeans and was bare-chested, fresh from the shower after a workout, enjoying a morning's reprieve from duty.

In a few clicks he was online and typed in the words 'Erica Ford statistical sociologist' and pressed the Enter key. The results were an unsatisfying page of links to articles on statistics by people by the name of Ford or Erika. He refined his search and simply entered 'Erica Ford'. The results spanned dozens of pages of links and he scanned them briefly before honing in on the one that caught his eye.

```
      Personnel details. Central University
                     offices.
   Erica Ford. Administrator. Department of
             Earth Sciences. Ext 5622
```

Connor sat back and scratched his head. He went back to the search page and entered 'statistical sociologist'. The results showed a few articles arguing whether sociology should require statistics and some links to courses in combined sociology, economics and statistics; nothing that would immediately confirm the existence of the discipline of statistical sociology.

He smiled and took a note of Erica's number.

TEN

Erica's birthday fell at the beginning of July by which time her spirits had lifted considerably. She had a date in her diary for the following week to meet up with Connor, and Carmi had generously made plans for them to spend a day at a health spa. She had taken to visiting the brewery regularly after work and had offered to do some of the year-end paper work for Harry to ease things in the office while staff took leave. Erica had been careful not to clash too much with Harry's own work schedule and had had an awkward conversation with his secretary when persuading her that she was able to lock up the brewery when others had left. Harry was a keyholder but Erica was not and staff were not easily swayed to bend company rules.

Erica gritted her teeth in anticipation of the meal that her father had arranged, aware that if the sun did not shine, they would surely all go mad together in the house for the day. Fortunately, the fine weather had not broken and Erica prepared the table in the garden and filled an old paddling pool for the twins.

Ellen arrived first, alone, tearing up the gravel in her new Audi cabriolet and bearing flowers and gifts of jewellery for Erica and wine for Harry. Janice arrived late with the twins and Cleo but without Keith, who she claimed, was needed for cricket.

The twins presented Erica with flowers and Cleo, a CD that was never likely to inspire her step aunt but which was gratefully received nonetheless.

Harry had been busy all morning and produced a large risotto and salad from the kitchen. The girls stood around the table, clutching wine glasses, Cleo giggling after a few sips.

"Well, find a seat, here we go." Said Harry setting the food down on the table.

Janice ushered the boys over and sat them between her and Cleo to administer their meal.

"Are you boys going to sit with your granddad?" Asked Harry patting the spare seat beside him. Casper looked up at his mum and frowned and Benedict stabbed at his plate with his fork, unspeaking.

"No, they'll sit with me." Said Janice and started to dish risotto onto their plates. Cleo shot an awkward smile across the table to Harry and fidgeted in her seat.

"I don't like mushrooms mummy." Benedict whined and pushed his plate away.

Cleo leant down and spoke quietly. "Just eat the rice and bread then. C'mon. I'll help you pick the mushrooms out."

Erica felt desperate for her father and the relationship he evidently craved with his grandsons. There was little connection there despite his efforts. The boys had been kept out of reach to the detriment of his forming a bond with them – some indomitable pursuit on Janice's part she figured, to agitate their father.

Erica stood up. "Cleo, will you swap with dad?" She asked.

"Sure." Said Cleo hesitantly. She slid her chair back slowly, squeezing Benedict's shoulder as she rose.

This one challenging request was a first for Erica. It was a blatant and unremorseful act of defiance targeted at Janice that sent a shockwave around the table. Ellen fiddled nervously with her rings and kept her eyes low. Harry moved in a slow dance with Cleo around the table. Erica continued to stand patiently, eyes wide, watching anxiety embed itself like shrapnel in her family. Janice was shamed, tearing bread for the twins with clammy hands.

Erica topped up everyone's glasses unnecessarily and Harry beamed at her from across the table — she was his ally — but Erica ignored him, unwilling to kindle the fire any further.

"This is a good Pinot." Said Ellen in a calculated attempt to steer the conversation onto a more benign subject. There was good food, good wine and a beautiful place to be sitting to enjoy it all. The presence of two four-year-olds at the table raised the atmosphere with their random questions and a kind of harmony was restored. They remained content with polite conversation until the twins' attention wandered.

"Your eyebrows are like caterpillars granddad." Said Benedict, and he reached up to touch Harry's face giggling. Harry leant forward evidently delighted at his grandson's interest and moved his fluffy white brows one at a time. The boys squealed and pulled back, cheeks high and eyes squinting.

"They *are* caterpillars!" Shrieked Caspar and reached up to touch them for himself. They exploded into laughter again and Harry continued to move them on demand.

Janice noisily pushed her chair away from the table announcing that she would clear up the plates. She was largely ignored, everyone else wrapt in the moment of the repeating routine of the caterpillar brows. She stacked the plates against each other loudly, scraping the boys' leftovers onto the top of the stack with unnecessary vigour.

"Boys, why don't you go and play in the paddling pool?" She asked. They ignored her but she stood her ground. "Caspar, Ben. Mummy's speaking to you." She boomed. They boys' laughter diminished and they looked up. "Go on now, the grown ups have got things they want to discuss."

"Janice! It's Erica's birthday." Ellen hissed. "Let it go."

"What things?" Asked Erica who had at last started to enjoy the emerging convivial nature of the afternoon.

"Nothing, nothing." Said Ellen dismissively. And then quickly. "What's for dessert dad?"

Erica could see that Harry was looking uncomfortable and that he was doing a poor job of hiding his knowledge of a subject Janice clearly wanted to raise. Mercifully, Benedict broke the silence.

"Granddad, will you come to the paddling pool too?"

Janice broke in. "No, granddad's staying here. Cleo will go with you. Now run along."

"But what's for pudding?" Benedict was whining now.

"We'll call you over when it's ready. Off you go." Janice gave a forced, matronly smile and pulled their chairs away from the table. The boys slid down awkwardly and padded out into the garden, Cleo in tow.

Ellen, on guard against an argument, glared at her older sister for having ignored her request to let the subject drop. Janice pushed the plates to the end of the table and sat down again. She spoke in a sing-song voice, out of synch with her previous manner. "Now, this won't take long I'm sure." She said, a statement that was as naïve as it was untrue.

Ellen rolled her eyes.

"What won't take long? What's going on?" Asked Erica, her face paling. "Is someone ill? Is it Aunt Dot?" She looked at Ellen. "Francoise?"

"No, no." Said Ellen, shaking her head. "No one's ill."

"Then what? Stop freaking me out."

Harry stretched his arms and gripped his chair with both hands looking down all the while. He looked like someone that was about to be sentenced for a crime and Erica thought she could feel him shrinking down inside himself.

Janice finally spoke, smooth and calculated. "As you know, this place..." She looked up towards the roof of the house and moved her arm in a vague semi circle. "Belonged to mum's parents – our grandparents – who left it to her in their will. In turn, mum left it to the four of us in *her* will." She turned to address Erica. "And, well, obviously that's never been an issue before now because you've needed a roof over your head et cetera, and you were just a teenager when she died but ..."

Ellen broke into a series of sneezes, which forced Janice to stop for a moment.

Erica cut in. "So you want your share now?"

Janice smoothed her hair behind her ears and pressed her skirt down on her lap with her hands, collecting herself from the directness of Erica's question.

"Not just me Erica, Ellen too. And it's not all about the money, it's about moving on. You'd get your share too if we sold this place – it must be worth a few bob. You could buy your *own* property, go travelling maybe, any number of things."

"But you've already got a house, a big one." Said Erica, her voice high and thin, feeling all at once the baby of the family in an adult conversation. She turned to Ellen. "And you've got your flat."

Ellen was familiar with Janice's methods of dragging her into family politics, but her direct reference to her agreement to the idea was incredible to her.

"I do, yes... and I'm not really all that fussed with what we do with this place..." Her voice tailed off.

Erica looked to Harry for some reassurance that the whole topic of conversation was news to him, but was disappointed to see his grey eyes dim and blank. She had always had an awareness that the house belonged to them all equally but had never challenged the idea that it would remain in the family, or more specifically, that her father would inhabit it for the rest of his life. In a second she contemplated the value of the place: a hundred thousand, a million? No matter what, divided by four it would be a tidy sum. Where would she buy a place of her own and where would Harry go? Would he have to retire to a flat in the city or some soulless new build in one of the larger village developments? He certainly couldn't afford to buy in Brenly especially if he was about to retire.

The sound of the boys shrieking and splashing in the paddling pool invaded everyone's thoughts, their laughter breaking the small discontented silence.

"OK, right. So you've all been discussing this already then?" Asked Erica addressing them all. "No. Don't answer that." She held her hands up and then placed them flat on the table. "Well I've been thinking about the house lately too as a matter of fact."

Janice gave Erica a shy *I knew you'd come round* smile and Harry's eyes fell to the table again.

"It is kind of stuck in the past, there's loads of old stuff knocking about in there, rooms we never use any more, books that haven't been touched for decades... just *stuff* really, clutter. The walls are covered – every square inch – I love your paintings dad, don't get me wrong, but all those weird old portraits are spooky. And the downstairs bathroom hasn't been touched in years." She paused, unsure where she was heading.

A large black cloud that had been casting a shadow pushed quietly out of view and the renewing warmth of the emerging sun relaxed her back into her stream of consciousness.

"It can get a bit spooky in there at times, cold almost, so I was thinking maybe redecorate downstairs, have a clear out, brighten the place up, and well…. advertise for a lodger."

Harry's eyebrows rose up into his forehead so far that his hair seemed to move down towards them. Erica pushed her chair back from the table, balancing it on two legs.

"Which I guess means that if you *did* want your share Janice, then dad and I would have some income to help pay for the money we'd need to borrow."

It was a conclusion to the matter that no one at the table had expected, not even Erica to some extent. She had surprised herself at her own confidence in airing a plan that had, up until that point, been a fleeting contemplation. It all seemed like a good idea: get someone into the house, a lively presence, someone young; stave off the unease of putting the key in the front door of a dark old house on a winter's evening.

Janice was poleaxed.

"Don't do that just for me." She looked at Ellen, wary that she may have no allies left. "I think it would be a great idea to get a lodger too, but please don't borrow money on my part. I just wanted you to be aware of the options Erica, that you don't have to stay here forever. And I just wanted to be able to send the boys to a private school in September, that's all."

Ellen, guilty for her repudiation of Janice's idea, cocked her head and murmured kindly. "But if dad and Erica got a lodger without borrowing any money, you could use the rent to do just that."

"Yeah, good idea." Said Erica, pleased at what was unfolding. "Problem solved." They waited for Harry's comment, Erica encouraging him by the slightest tilt of her head.

"Yes, I'd be amenable to that." He said slowly. Then directly to Janice. "If you are love."

"Yes, that's fine." Janice snapped. "See, that didn't take long did it? I'll just get the boys for dessert." Ellen moved swiftly to accompany her, slipping her arm inside Janice's as they walked into the garden.

When they were out of earshot, Erica leant over the table and spoke with gritted teeth. "What is it with you two?" Harry's look of contentment melted. "I can't bear it dad, I really can't. You've got to sort it out."

Harry was taken aback. Erica's suggestion suddenly felt like the application of a band aid to an amorphous, unpredictable wound. It was, however, the easy option.

"Oh… it… well, she's… yes… uh…"

Caspar and Benedict ran back to the table and went straight to Harry, tugging his sleeves and asking for dessert. He led them both into the kitchen, each of his bony hands placed gently on their heads. Erica thought that her heart might break for the dysfunction that was her family. By the time Harry emerged with rhubarb crumble – a dessert that resounded through Erica's whole childhood – Janice and Ellen were still walking about the garden. Erica swallowed down a meagre helping, and with it, the lubrication of her own salty tears in her throat.

Connor Fairchild, who was a high-ranking officer in the police force for his age, was quiet by nature. His notoriety at work for accuracy and commitment to the job at hand, had gained him a respect worthy of the effort he put in. At thirty-four, and after ten years of focussing on his career, he felt an itch within him to try something else. He'd attended evening classes and had even taken a few rudimentary flying lessons but couldn't see himself as a commercial or military pilot and had returned to part time study in subjects less vocational.

He had been contentedly single for a year – following a particularly gritty end to his previous relationship – and was happy to pursue new possibilities without haste.

He arranged to meet with Erica on neutral territory over lunch the week after her birthday. Erica's request remained something of a mystery to him still, and while he was doubtful as to her integrity as an academic researcher, he felt drawn to her in a way that was beyond basic physical attraction. It had taken them so long since their encounter in Brenly village hall to actually meet up that he had all but given up hope of seeing her again; the intensity of the investigation of the crimes in Brenly had waned and with it, his visits to Brenly itself. Her call had come as something of a surprise to him and he had been disappointed by the irregular shift patterns of the summer months, preventing their liaison from occurring sooner.

He sat outside the Bend in the River pub, checking his watch and enjoying the sun on his skin. Erica was on time and Connor spotted her gingerly walking down the steps to the beer garden wearing a smart blue dress and a pair of oversized sunglasses that dominated her face.

He stood up and waved. Erica walked over slowly and with some apparent difficulty, in a pair of high wedge sandals, clutching a glass of lime and soda. They shook hands firmly and settled into an easy exchange of formalities regarding the menu, the setting of the pub on the riverbank and the fine weather. They ordered food and dithered around subjects of no consequence.

"That's just a few things I printed for you last week." Connor said, pushing a small stack of papers across the table. "I couldn't remember exactly what it was you were after so I'm sorry if it's a bit off the mark."

"No, that's great, thank you." Said Erica sweetly.

"It's all publicly available. If you know where to look that is. Information on crime is needed for community reasons anyway. Burglaries and car crime are easy figures to get hold of. Any officer can request this information internally without question. Numbers are fine to dish out but no specifics. No people or names." He smiled. "Ask me anything you like though. I'll do my best."

"Thank you. Yes I will." Erica pulled a small hardbound notebook and a biro from her bag and set them down on the table. He eyed her movements, always fiddling with her pen or her glass, the regular crossing and uncrossing of her legs.

"You look just like your dad you know." Connor's eyes narrowed as he smiled and he glimpsed at Erica bashfully."

"D-do I?"

"Same hair, tall and slim, y'know."

"Well, yes, some people say I do. Without the grey hair. Obviously." She laughed nervously.

"And without such an interest in brewing beer too I'm sure." Connor laughed at his own remark, raised his glass in salute to the general reference of brewing beer, and took a sip.

"Well, actually I do know a little bit. Dad's been at it for forty years so it's kind of hard to ignore." Erica cleared her throat. "How did you know about dad and the brewery?" She asked cheerfully.

"We've had to learn about a lot of the Brenly folk during the investigation. But also because I took my parents to the brewery to do the tour a few years ago when they were over. I think it was your dad who took us round. He's an interesting man. Knows a lot about the industry."

A waitress emerged from the pub with two plates. Connor was grateful for the distraction and set about describing the kind of food available to him at the police station. His description of soggy chips and solid pastry made Erica laugh casually and chide him for what must surely be an exaggeration.

"When did you come to England?" She asked impassively between mouthfuls of food.

"I came over when I was twenty-one. Followed a girl. We moved here together when she went to college. Then things went wrong after a few years. She went back when she graduated and I stayed here 'cos I sort of fell in love with the place. There's five in my family back home, so I don't think my folks miss me all that much. They're busy with the grandchildren now anyway. Plus two of my brothers are a bit *political* shall we say, and never really approved of my career. There's no love lost between us though I do miss them from time to time, especially my sister Niamh. She's great, you'd really like her."

Connor produced a worn black wallet from his pocket.

"Here." He said shifting his chair nearer to Erica's and pulling out a few creased photographs. "This is Niamh, her boyfriend Daniel – he was a friend of mine at school – my folks... and this is all of us at my little brother's wedding last year."

"Gosh, you're all so tall and, well..."

"Bald!" Added Connor.

"Oh, no... well..." There was nothing to be contested in this fact concerning the men in the Fairchild family and Erica giggled with him. "Niamh's very pretty." She added. "She looks most similar to you."

"Yes, we were always called the twins when we were wee."

Connor doubted that Erica's intentions for their meeting were ever entirely professional although he wondered if this idle chat about his family might be making her feel uncomfortable.

"Anyway, I'm sure you're not interested in all this stuff." He said and slipped the photographs back into his wallet. He shuffled his chair back round and continued with his lunch.

"No, no, not at all." Said Erica encouragingly. "I mean, I am interested... I'm not *not* interested... is what I meant."

Connor smiled. He was satisfied that he still liked Erica as he had first done. She was tall with the potential for elegance, obviously intelligent but like a fish out of water on some social fronts, bumbling, curious and anxious to please.

"Good, good." He said. "So are you going to ask me some questions then? What did you say you did for a job – you're at the university aren't you?"

Erica dabbed her mouth, pushed her plate to one side and reached for her note book.

"I'm looking for some statistics really, on crime in the area, but by that I mean in detail. Not just the county, but segments of the county, parishes, small communities... if you have that sort of information."

"I do." Said Connor formally. "Depends on what sort of crime."

"Violent crime, committed by men, whether that's just aggressive behaviour or real heavy stuff... erm... the bad things. I don't want the details of the crimes, just numbers, maybe over the next six months or so."

"Right, well, you know that with the Freedom of Information Act that a lot of this stuff is available, minus names and addresses of course. And there's a world of difference between aggressive behaviour and violent crime so there'd be quite a bit to sift through."

"Yes... uh... yes. But it was perhaps more of a personal take on things in addition that I thought you might be able to help me with. An overview, trends."

"OK. But why the next six months particularly?"

Erica took a sip of her drink and choked as it went down the wrong way. Connor rose nimbly and patted her back as she coughed and her face reddened. It was a few minutes before her voice was recovered and she squeaked an unnecessary apology. Connor absently left his hand resting between her shoulder blades for a while longer and Erica laughed nervously. Normality restored, he waited for her to pick up the question.

"The six month thing." She began, her voice small. "Is just because the study – uh, my study – has to cover a particular period of time. That's all, it's just a formality really."

Sitting close up to each other, their faces betrayed the intimate observations they were making: the smell of their breath, the undulations of their skin.

"I'm looking at possible correlations between people who live near electricity pylons and levels of violence." She continued. "Not actually *at* the site of the pylons themselves – no, that would be…weird – but those people who live near them. How it might affect them."

Connor considered this plausible enough in the wide gamut of research he'd come across in the past. It was an unusual project, but it wasn't entirely unfeasible.

"And you want me to do what… exactly?"

"Well – only if you don't mind – erm… provide some information on individuals or maybe groups."

Connor pulled his drink over from the other side of the table, thinking earnestly about this request for a moment. He sipped and turned to face Erica, resting his chin on his hand and squinting in the sun.

"I can help you with some general stats really, give you my take on things… but that's all."

"OK yes, that's fine. Absolutely."

"It's OK though." He said quickly. "Just give me the names of the places you had in mind and I'll see what I can do."

"OK. Thanks."

"And what is this study exactly? Is it part of your job or something you've got going on the side?"

Connor's question had slipped out because he was burning to ask it but it carried with it the future integrity of their relationship: it would test whether Erica was bright enough to have explored the possibility that Connor might know more about her than he was letting on and it would reveal to him a fundamental detail of trust required if he was to pursue their friendship any further.

Erica finished her drink and drained the last of the sweet liquid from melting ice cubes. She turned her head to one side and looked him full in the eyes.

"It's a project." She said. "It's not for work. Please don't ask me any more than that, if you don't mind – it's quite boring really."

Connor was satisfied, relieved.

"No worries. I'm no stranger to part-time study. I've been grappling with distance education for a few years myself. The project work is always the hardest to get motivated with, so fair play to you. I'll look forward to reading the finished product. Is it a college course you're doing in the evenings or—"

"Oh my god!" Exclaimed Erica ducking animatedly. "That's my ex."

"Where?"

"On the bridge. Up there." Erica nodded." In the chinos, leaning over."

Connor looked up and saw Duncan on the bridge that was busy with cars, bicycles and pedestrians. He was one of a few strollers taking the time to stop and look at the river and the boats moored up beneath it. He was wearing sunglasses making it impossible to tell if he was looking back at them from forty feet, although his body was inclined away slightly.

"Do you mean the one with the ankle flappers, the chubby bald guy?"

Erica nodded.

"Oh my god, you went out with *him*!" Connor burst into a low infectious giggle. "But he's so... *nerdy*..."

"But so am I." Erica laughed nervously. "So am *I*."

"But he's so square, he's practically a cube."

Erica rested her forehead on the table and rocked with laughter. "That's mean. He's really sweet."

"How long were you with him?"

"Three years. Or thereabouts."

"Three years! Holy moly."

Erica glanced at her watch and gasped – she had to leave immediately for the office.

They thanked each other for an enjoyable lunch and Erica packed her as yet unsoiled notebook back into her bag. Connor made a promise that he'd be in touch and the bones of a plan were laid for a ride out to a pub sometime.

As she walked back in towards the centre of town, Erica called Carmi from her mobile phone and picked her way hastily through the crowds. Twenty feet behind her, in long deliberate strides, Duncan Okolski followed along in the same path.

ELEVEN

August in Brenly was a time to lower the pace of life. Hollyhocks appeared in shocks of pink and orange at a time when the best of the summer's blooms had faded. In the garden of the Old Rectory, the white orbs of feverfew had withered and the poppy heads were reduced to smooth brown pods, their edges like the folds of a Cornish pasty. The purple clematis was gearing up for its second bloom and the first of the Japanese anemones rose up alongside a late flourish of roses. Ornamental thistles that stood in clumps by the greenhouse were awash with bumblebees pulling their heads down with every sup, their bodies as fat as the thistle-heads they dined on. Bottles and beer cans were plucked from around the park benches by disapproving early morning dog walkers and the school playgrounds were quiet save for the morning of exam results. Children's voices came out with the sunshine and the pavements were home to rudimentary cricket matches and the eager clatter of bicycles.

Driving in and out of the village was a forced amble; even the younger speed merchants were reduced to third gear to take in the sight of the cutting and stacking of the wheat. The late evening shadows on the fields turned hay rolls into immaculately spaced cylinders in broad open fields, the sumptuous golden light exacerbating the blacks and blues of ravens that gathered there.

The odd downpour kept the lawn from disintegrating entirely and Harry busy to keep it shorn. Runner beans had produced their first stringy pods, tomatoes had set and golden plums ripened and fell in a few days, keeping Erica occupied in a cycle of picking, stewing and freezing.

Against this backdrop, Erica was tied up in knots about Connor. She slipped quickly from feelings of regret about Duncan, to anxiety relating to the premise on which her friendship with Connor was based. August was the time of year when it was impossible to ignore revisiting resolutions laid for the year that were not yet realised and the first drop of charity Christmas card brochures arrived through the door with depressing timing. Erica had annual leave to take but no one to take it with and had opted instead for extended weekends and odd days here and there to redecorate parts of the house.

Three events defined the month of August of that year for Erica Ford, the imagined consequences of which she kept firmly in her mind without so much as a whisper to Carmi, Harry or her sisters.

The first was a weekend at Janice's looking after Caspar and Benedict while Janice and Keith were away. Erica had found time on her hands in the evening when the boys were asleep. With nothing much of interest to watch on TV, she'd padded about the place and settled down to pick through an old bookcase. A dog-eared photograph album had caught her eye and not recognising it, she leafed through it crossed legged on the floor. It was an album that contained photos of the whole family in the seventies and eighties, some of which Erica had never seen before. After turning only a few leaves, it struck her that there were no pictures of Harry, or if it was obvious that Harry had been in a photo, his presence had been removed by the artful slice of Janice's scissors.

Erica had moved faster through the album and had been horrified to find at the end that her fathers' presence amounted to little more than the back or side of his head in backgrounds. She had spent the night on the sofa uncomfortably turning this over in her head, imagining all sorts of events – most of them sinister and alarming – that would have incited such a dislike of her father by Janice.

A downpour had kept her awake until dawn and she had eventually woken at ten with sunlight on her face, sweating and cramped under a lumpy duvet.

She'd ambled upstairs to locate the boys and had been concerned to find their beds empty. After a dash around the house Erica had thrown on some boots and marched outside. The boys were sitting at the end of the garden, long green fishing nets in hand, perched on some hefty rocks that marked the boundary of the garden with a shallow stream.

"There you are." She had said, relieved to find them so content and amused with their own company. She had gently chided them for wandering off and tried to coax them in to get dressed for breakfast. They hadn't wanted to budge so Erica had joined them, balancing on a chunk of limestone in lilac pyjamas.

"We're waiting for the King of the Otters when we sit here." Benedict had said. "One day he'll come and take us away."

"But it will be OK." Caspar had added brightly. "It'll be lovely and like floating and it will make us feel all nice inside."

"Like when you're falling asleep."

"He'll pick us up from the stream. He'll come down and we'll swim away with him."

"And we won't come back." Ben had concluded and glanced briefly up at his aunt, his reddish brown locks diaphanous in the sunlight.

Erica had been dumbfounded by the metaphor she thought was being relayed to her by her two four-and-a-half year-old nephews. Granted, they were bright for their age and serious with it, but it was a bit much to expect them to take on concepts of life and death at their stage in life.

"Who is the King of the Otters?" She had asked gently. Absorbed with dipping their nets in to the stream Benedict had eventually spoken, the bolder of the two.

"He's what took Cleo's mummy away."

"And mummy's mummy." Caspar had added.

Neither of them had looked at Erica, they had seemed sad in their play and yet fixed by the movement of the stream and the promise of what it might bring. Erica had run her hands through her hair pulling it into a knot off her face and thought about what she might say next. The decent thing would be to clap her hands and bring in to the conversation the plan for the day: breakfast, games and a trip to the swings, but instead she had gone with a more devious desire to pursue the topic further.

"But you don't want to be taken away by... the King of the Otters... do you?" She had asked, stroking the hair on Benedict's head. "Not now. And waiting for him here won't make him come any quicker either."

"Cleo said that you don't know when he's going to come." Benedict had said brightly. "But he is bea-u-t-i-ful... and strong. But also shiny like a light."

"Mummy said that when her mummy went away with him it was because granddad had called him." Caspar had said earnestly.

With this Erica had stood up and ruffled the boys' hair. The horror of their revelation had made her nauseous. "C'mon." She had said. "We're going in now. I'm making scrambled eggs and then we're off to the park."

"Yeah!" Screamed Caspar and had taken off from his perch to run in circles on the lawn waving his net above his head, his pyjamas soaked by the wet grass.

When Cleo had returned later that afternoon, Erica had tentatively raised the subject with her. She had responded in an off-hand manner referring to it as '*that old story*' and had drifted up to her room, to nurse what Erica perceived to be a hangover.

The second event that had defined the month of August for Erica was an afternoon spent cycling with Connor in the Cotswolds. It had been made all the more pleasant in Erica's view because they had steered clear of the subject of the attacks in Brenly, Connor's work and Erica's project, and instead talked about the things they observed on their journey, remembrances of their childhood, snippets of their lives past and their desires for the future. Politics and religion had even appeared briefly and agreeably on the agenda. Erica had felt free, cocky, enjoying the sun on her skin, voicing her opinions and confident in new summer clothes that Carmi had chosen for her.

It had suited her that they wouldn't see each other for a while, Connor making excuses for being tied up at a wedding and extended holiday in Italy with friends. It had added an element of freedom to the day – a certain antithesis of urgency to their friendship – that neither were tied specifically to each other nor counting the days until their next meeting. She hadn't needed to justify herself, talk about her family as such, just act and feel for the moment in good company; it was the kind of afternoon she had craved for her and Duncan but which had never transpired over the course of three years. It jarred her for this revelation and was something she kept coming back to over the following days and weeks.

The third defining event had come towards the end of August when humidity and showers had become the meteorological norm. Wasps had hung in agitated rhythms by fallen fruit and sunflower heads stooped in osteoporitic arcs. Erica had just finished painting the downstairs bathroom: boxes of books and oddments were stacked in the hallway, ready to begin a new life in the loft or on the shelves of a charity shop. Being in all day, she had been listening to music and had not taken in the news or so much as looked out of the window since breakfast.

Harry had come home earlier than usual in his overalls and had inspected Erica's handiwork, praising her efforts. He had ushered her into the kitchen and put the kettle on, hovering over the teapot, agreeing a suitable course of action for acquiring a lodger.

Then came the blow.

"Erica, there's been another… burglary. This time in Malmsbury Ditton. Last night it was. I don't know the family – surname of Penfold so I'm told – only this time it was a bit worse."

"Oh?" She had sat obediently opposite her father and listened. Malmsbury Ditton was only six or seven miles away.

Harry had opened a biscuit tin, placed it on the kitchen table and sat down opposite her.

"I spoke to the police on the way here, they were stopping people on the Thame Road." He had paused to dip a ginger nut in his tea. Erica had sat patiently, her hands clammy in her lap.

"It was another burglary, only this time the burglar didn't seem to really care about who was in the house, not like last time. He pushed the couple into the cellar 'pparently and locked the door. Then he nicked a load of stuff – specific pieces it would seem – clocks, jewellery, valuables, that sort of thing. But he was nasty Erica, rough with the couple… aggressive. They were a bit bruised but otherwise OK."

Erica had listened intently, her eyes wide, concentrating on Harry's story.

"Police were saying that it was well planned but because he didn't speak as such, they still don't have a lead on where he might originally be from." Harry had sipped at his tea and continued quietly. "So there's talk of everyone having DNA tests if they can find one of his hairs or whatnot left in the house, something to identify him by. Seems like a good idea don't you think?"

"I just can't believe that he hasn't been found." Erica had said. "What are there – five thousand people in Brenly? Everyone knows everyone, including the farming families outside. Surely someone behaving oddly would have been spotted by now?"

"It does seem ridiculous love, I'll grant you that. I heard that a similar spate happened a few years ago in the Gloucester area. The thieves were from Birmingham but travelled down regularly to target a specific village to give the illusion that it was someone local. They honed in on the bigger houses then too. It could be, you know, one of those copycat crimes. Maybe the perpetrator's not even from round here. Who knows?" Harry had shrugged his shoulders and sipped from his cup. "Point is love, the sooner we get a lodger in here the better. I won't be happy until I know that there's a bit more life to this place when I'm not around, that you've got company in the evenings. And I've asked Stan to come back next weekend to lop more off the trees at the front. Makes no sense there being so many dark places out there."

"Places to hide." Erica had added sadly. "I'd been thinking the same thing."

"I just don't know what motivates these sorts of people. What are they going to do with all that stuff? Make a few bob I suppose and then have a rotten conscience for the rest of their lives.

"But hurting people in the process… that's just… unnecessary." He had looked into Erica's eyes and said sternly. "And I don't want no one hurting you love." He had reached out for her hand over the table.

"I know dad, I know. Nor do I. Men are just like that though: angry, pointlessly obsessed with causing harm some of them – *driven*. It bothers me dad. When you've been on the receiving end…. It's the same all over the world, unless you're looking at a disaster of an environmental nature, the wars, the torture, the religious battles, it all starts with men. Men at the top of every religion, men at the top of every superpower, throwing their weight around."

Harry had frowned and sat back. "You're beginning to sound like your sister." He had stood up and ruffled her hair, reaching for the kettle to top up the pot. "We build pretty good bridges too you know and brew damn fine beer if I'm not mistaken." He had sat down again and Erica smiled weakly at him. "And let's not forget Maggie in your little equation. She sank the Belgrano single-handedly—"

"Yes, yes, apart from Thatch, although she is practically a man in many ways…"

"Or that one in the Philippines with all those hats. Whatshername…?"

"Imelda Marcos. And she had shoes not hats…"

And so the conversation had gone on, with each imparting varying degrees of accuracy in their knowledge of the great and the bad men and women of history.

They'd stayed close together that evening, putting the finishing touches to the spare room and shifting boxes into the loft.

TWELVE

Aside the thick oak balustrade of the viewing gallery, the only thing that stood between Erica and the task at hand, was the illegality of her intentions. Deception, perfidy and a disregard for common decency lingered in the back of her mind and in the undulations of her guts. But they did not obstruct her view; the only true barrier was the actual presence of brewery staff at the wrong time which she dealt with promptly.

It was the Sunday after the summer bank holiday, Harry was out west visiting his sister and the brewery was quiet save for the hum of only one of the fermentation tanks. In the brewery calendar, it was the calm before the storm: a five-day-a-week schedule that would increase to six or seven come the autumn to accommodate Christmas orders. The first brew of the day started at five in the morning finishing at midday, the second finishing at four in the afternoon followed by the clean-up, and so on. The fermentation tanks were never without action, some beers taking up to four days to ferment, though when the rest of the brewery was silent they required irregular checks and could be left at length at weekends.

Erica knew the cycle of checks on the tanks. She could get access to the brewing schedules, she knew the staff who worked the shifts and she knew where the resultant beer would be heading for despatch. Late that afternoon she had brazenly strolled in, announcing to a new apprentice, Saul, that she would be completing some paperwork in the offices. She offered to check on the tank herself if he wanted to knock off early before his replacement arrived that evening. Saul accepted her offer without hesitation and Erica bolted the main door after him.

She walked down the stairs one at a time, her knees weak. In trainers and loose-fitting jeans, her hair was tied into a bulky knot on her head and a large brown rucksack was slung over her shoulder. It contained the packages of ground up medicine that had been sitting under her bed since May, labelled in a rough hand – *fertilizer* – should she be run over by a bus and her possessions scrutinised.

Her calculation had been swift: fermentation at sixteen degrees Celsius was not hot enough to dissolve the powder and so it would need to be incorporated into an earlier stage of the brewing process. The gristing – the crushing of barley – and heating of the resultant 'mash' was undertaken the night before a brew and at a temperature of up to seventy degrees Celsius which would adequately dissolve the powder. The scheduled beer was the sweetest that the brewery manufactured and they had an order for two hundred barrels for a group of Oxfordshire pubs. Harry had always maintained that connoisseurs never went for the sweeter beers; they were undoubtedly aimed at the less refined palette. This then was the safest bet for contamination: Joe Bloggs was less likely to notice a difference.

The enormity of what Erica was about to do rolled over her in thick guilty waves. The undulations of the concrete floor seemed to shift into new forms and she steadied herself on the banister making her way down. The largest of the fermentation tanks – Anakin – quietly spewed froth the colour of polluted sea water down its sides. The bubbles burst and dark brown liquid trickled into the drains.

Erica stood at the foot of the stairs and inhaled deeply to take in the bready odour as sustenance for the task before her. She walked slowly past Anakin towards a wall of white nylon barley sacks, bulging and dusty, and stopped to touch one of them. The tick of the factory clock knocked at her skull and the thump of her heart shook her ears; she swallowed to release the pressure in her head.

To her right were sacks of hop pellets, green and pungent, the topmost split and its contents exposed, delivering a sharp lemony odour to the air that drew Erica towards it. She slid her bag off her shoulder and lowered her face towards the sack, closing her eyes for a moment.

A single pellet crushed in the fingers stayed on the skin like an acrid geranium until scrubbed away. Dorothy had used them to invigorate potpourri around the house or crushed them into a hot bath in the winter, a ritual that had delighted Harry and that the girls had taken for granted when growing up. It was a smell of times past, out of place somehow, relived now in its practical setting.

Erica opened her eyes. At the far end of the brewery, the two enormous copper kettles stood silent and shiny, anxious for ignition. She looked to her right, past the hefty oblong yeast culturing vessels and finally to the mash tub. It was a soulless steel vessel held up on four sturdy legs, with a capacity for two hundred barrels of liquid at a time. Beneath it, a spaghetti of wide pipes at various stages of corrosion, white painted taps and glass dials.

The mash tub was her target. Sterilised and ready for the next brew, it would be easy to slip the powder in. No one was expected to look inside the thing before it was heated up and the water and mash added. It was that or the grist mill whose guts were more visible from eye level.

Erica picked up her rucksack, walked quickly over to the mash tub and silently climbed a set of small iron stairs. She peered into the huge metal container via a small chute used to test the consistency of the brew: it was empty, dry and ready for work.

Erica slowly unzipped her bag.

A wood pigeon that had been sitting idle in the steel rafters, swooped down from its perch moving gracelessly from above the main entrance. It dropped low over Erica's head and came to rest on top of one of the copper kettles. She gasped and her impulse to duck as the bird flew over was immediate and unconscious. The interruption brought her up short. She peered towards the main entrance of the brewing hall and scanned the pile of empty barrels and pallets. The main door was still bolted. Her ears strained to hear past the clock and the hum of Anakin, but there was nothing else to hear save for the whoosh of cars passing in the street outside. Erica looked around her for another minute, eyes wide, mouth dry.

How harmful could this speculative quackery really be? The doses she had calculated that would be administered would be so small that they would not elicit a change in the taste of the beer. Drinking several pints in one go, or several pints over a series of days – for the hardened consumer – might make some discernable difference to the recipient: a good one, not so much to tranquilise but to make unexcitable. There were no major side effects that she was aware of, nothing in the literature that yelled 'risk of heart failure' or 'stroke'. It was a prophylaxis for aggression on a par with adding fluoride to drinking water to prevent tooth decay. Simple, probably harmless and hopefully effective.

Erica's internal casuistic digression distracted her from the task at hand. She looked up at the bird who blinked back at her, back to the main entrance, the barrels and up to the viewing gallery.

Relative calm.

"Here goes." She whispered.

She pulled out the dozen or so bags of powder from the rucksack, untied them hastily and poured them down the chute. When they were emptied she peered into it and blew to dislodge any residue that might be stuck to the sides.

Job done. It has been so quick, so effortless.

She stuffed the empty plastic bags back into her rucksack and moved quickly away from the mash tub towards the viewing gallery. The pigeon made another agitated flight back to the rafters and Erica glanced up to watch its clumsy trajectory. She walked back up the oak stairs, her legs leaden, the tendons around her knees seeming to work against the muscles in her legs with every step.

Walking back into the offices, she made a beeline for her father's office and gingerly sat down. The security cameras relayed blinking black and white images of the yard, the gates and the brewing hall. She ran her fingers over the buttons on the cameras' console, pushed the one marked 'Record' from the *off* to the *on* position and sat back heavily in Harry's chair.

The fridge in the staff kitchen shuddered into life and Erica shifted at the desk unable to get comfortable. She pulled out a few papers that Harry had asked her to check – mainly advertising copy. It would be another hour before the staff for the next shift arrived and Erica was content to wait.

Harry woke up staring at the dusty chandelier that hung from the lounge ceiling. He inhaled deeply and blinked, confused and not recognising where he was. The disorientation experienced in those few moments sent his mind racing through a set of possibilities of not only identifying where he might be, but considering the reasons for this lapse in cognition: was he dreaming, was he losing his mind, or more specifically, was this the beginning of the end on some slippery slope to some awful hazy demise? He had lost track of where he was on the way home from work the other day; granted he had been tired from an exceptionally long shift, but still…

The doorbell rang urgently two or three times in succession and Harry sat up rubbing his head. He walked distractedly into the hall, bumping against the doorway en route. The heavy front door shuddered as he yanked it open, cursing its protestation against the undulations of the weather. A tall, handsome woman, somewhere in her early fifties, with bright eyes and heavy blue mascara, stood smiling on the doorstep.

"Hello." She said eagerly. "I'm Monique."

"Hi." Said Harry pushing his hair back off his forehead in a futile attempt to neaten up his dishevelment.

They stood for a second, Harry contemplating briefly through the haze of recently waking up, how most politely to ask the question – *what do you want?*

"Oh sorry. I rang a few times. I'm sorry if I disturbed you." She said in a light French accent. She rummaged awkwardly in a shiny gold-clasped handbag and pulled out a folded piece of paper. "I'm here to see the room. Errr… this is the Old Rectory?"

"Oh yes, of course. Sorry about that. Do come in." Harry opened the door fully and took a step back. "I've just come back from a trip and I'm a little tired from the journey. I totally forgot."

Monique stepped in and followed Harry deeper in to the hallway.

"You must be the one that left the message with my daughter." Harry caught a touch of sweet perfume as Monique passed him and let his eyes wander to the tightly packaged backside that inhabited Monique's knee-length trousers. She was smart in stilettos and a neat summer jacket, a thick blond bob elegantly coiffed around her neck.

"It is so beautiful. Such an interesting house." She said looking up at the portraits and still life that, whilst recently thinned out by Erica, still dominated the walls. "You kept the inside old as well as the outside." She said, her hands on her hips generously appraising the hall and peering along into the kitchen.

"Well, we try our best to keep it, you know, restored."

"We?" She turned to look Harry directly in the eyes.

"Me and my daughter – Erica. You spoke to her on the phone I think."

"Oh I see. Just the two of you here then."

"Yes, just the two of us."

Monique beamed and waited for Harry to elaborate on the matter.

"The room's just down here." He gestured to a door by the stairs.

They walked in to a small, freshly-painted room, furnished with an antique pine bed and a chest of drawers. Erica had put up new blinds against a small sash window that transmitted a bright beam of afternoon sunlight. It sliced the room in half, specs of dust visible in its path, floating like plankton in seawater. The overall effect was a feminine, uncluttered and welcoming space made quirky by a sloping ceiling and elaborate bedstead. Harry explained that the room had exclusive access to the downstairs bathroom but that kitchen facilities would be shared. Monique listened, nodding at appropriate intervals. She was quick to express a sincere interest in taking it and Harry led her out into the kitchen.

"It will suit me fine." She said. "I'm sort of in *in-between* circumstances at the moment. So I'm just looking for somewhere where I can collect my thoughts for a while you know? Without being… cut off."

"Yes, yes of course." Agreed Harry fiddling with milk and cups. "Well we sort of come and go to a regular rhythm, me and Erica. We both work full time but occasionally my shifts take me away from the normal nine to five."

"Oh, and what is it that you do?"

And so began a protracted interrogation of Harry into the details of his working life, of his hobbies and interests and of the house itself. He left little out, waxing at length about the brewery and willingly gave up more information than he might have done if faced with a man of the same age, or for that matter, someone altogether less attractive than Monique. By comparison, Monique revealed few facts about her personal circumstances, but enough to keep the conversation on an even keel.

She had left France twenty years ago and had married an Englishman. They were now divorced, without children and she was teaching French at a comprehensive school. She had given most of her career to working in deprived areas of Birmingham but had moved south for a less stressful job in a more rural setting.

By the time that Erica came home from work, they were into their second round of drinks (Monique sticking resolutely to fresh coffee) and had made inroads into a loaf of Jamaica ginger cake. Harry was gleefully recalling a family holiday in a gite in the south of France in the 1990s giving exaggerated accounts of the freshness of the local produce and the conviviality of the market traders they had encountered. The truth was that he had little recollection of the details of the holiday other than the fiasco caused by a rotten stair that had left him with splinters and deep scratches on his legs for weeks after he had fallen though it. He didn't hear Erica come in and was a little surprised when she appeared at the kitchen door.

"Ah Erica!" He said, expressing an energetic enthusiasm for her return home. "This is Monique. She's come to see the room. Well, actually, she'd like to take the room so we've been just having a chat and sorting things out."

Erica bade a friendly hello to Monique and they shook hands. Harry pulled a chair out for her to join them at the table and she hesitated before sitting down. That day, like most of her working days, she was dressed in decade-old flat leather shoes – polished, re-polished and re-soled – and a pair of loose black trousers. Her hair was in a similar state to Harry's in its wildness – a look that only those with tight curls dare to pull off – but that to the trained eye suggested that it hadn't been touched at all that day.

Erica seemed to shrink into the chair a little and Harry at once felt guilty for dragging her in to the conversation when she was evidently tired. He wittered on nonetheless, refuelling his daughter with cake and a mug of strong tea; Monique listened and smiled at appropriate intervals. By the time that the sun had set – a full hour later – the talk had slowed pace and had moved onto the practicalities of how and when Monique might move in. Harry's stomach was growling and he contemplated briefly the idea of inviting her to stay for dinner seeing as she appeared to be in no hurry to leave. Whilst she was visiting the bathroom he ran the idea past Erica who frowned back at him.

"Dad, I'm tired. Sorry. And besides, I want to hear about Aunt Dot."

"Ah. Yes. OK. Just thought I'd check."

Erica hauled herself up from the table continuing in a sigh. "We'll have to get the rugs put back down in the hall. I just put them up in the loft too."

"Why?"

"Those stilettos." Erica whispered, pointing vaguely in the direction of the bathroom.

"Oh, uh. Yes."

Erica took the opportunity to edge her way out of the kitchen to make a phone call. Within ten minutes of her return, Monique was graciously despatched by Harry into the cool September evening. He returned to the kitchen humming brightly and put the radio on. Erica slumped onto the sofa in the lounge, switched on the television, turning the volume up as far as was reasonable to drown it out.

THIRTEEN

The next day Erica tracked down Carmi at work and insisted that they meet for lunch. The main refectory was heaving with freshers and Erica groaned as she looked in.

"Let's just go for a walk." She said briskly. "C'mon." She took Carmi's arm and turned away from the door.

"What? In these shoes? I don't think so."

Erica eyed Carmi's stilettos and elicited an "Ah" that she hoped didn't sound too offensive.

"I know. You're thinking 'inappropriate for the office' and I'm thinking 'how long can one girl wear the same pair of shoes?'" Said Carmi nodding in the direction of Erica's feet.

"I'm at work. Who cares what shoes I've got on?"

Carmi raised her eyebrows but was cut short of a retort by being amply jostled by a pack of students.

"Excuse *me*." She boomed and Erica pulled her away from the doorway.

"The high street will be packed. Let's get a drink at the Pavilion."

"Fine." Said Erica. They headed away from the main thoroughfare and to the sports fields, arm in arm.

"I can't go hiking in these things, we'll have to walk more slowly. I only wear them for the shock factor. A kind of silent protest against the socks and sandals of the department." Explained Carmi.

"I'd hardly call it a *silent* protest."

Carmi nudged her friend amicably. "This better be good. "She said. "I've been in need of something juicy to get my head around, something other than this bloody paper I'm trying to finish by Friday. Clag Features had the audacity to suggest putting *his* name before mine when I showed him the final draft. Never mind the hypothesis, the days spent in the lab, the beautifully constructed arguments, his words were 'I think we're agreed I should be first author don't you? Might carry a little bit more weight.'" Said Carmi doing a poor job of a whiny Glaswegian accent.

'Clag Features' was, Erica assumed, Carmi's newest name for her former Ph.D. supervisor and someone with whom Carmi had had numerous, animated disputes over the years.

"More weight? I don't think so. More weight for what? I'm not exactly submitting to *Nature*. For a start the abstract's already been accepted and I met the editor at that conference in May and I know for a *fact* that he thinks Clag Features is a flaky old has-been who hasn't had an original thought since…. since… discussions around the cell biology equivalent of plate tectonics in the Sixties." Carmi inhaled expressively as if having forgotten to breathe during her speech.

Erica smiled. "The cell biology equivalent of plate tectonics?"

"Yeah, you know. Crack and Whitsun. The double helix. That sort of thing. Amino acids."

"Crick and Watson were the Fifties." Erica corrected assertively.

"Fifties, Sixties. A bloody long time ago anyway."

"And did he contribute to their work?"

Carmi frowned back at Erica's perplexed face in profile as they walked. "No, course not. That's the point."

It occurred to Erica that there was often a lack of logic associated with Carmi's amusing rants. In an attempt to be the jester she often lost the plot of what she was saying.

"Carmi, you don't half talk a load of crap sometimes for someone that's supposed to have *beautifully constructed* arguments."

"Oh oh oh." Carmi scalded. "You know what I mean. He wrote some dopey little paper about forty years ago on mitochondrial DNA which was *the* thing at the time – the plate tectonics reference was just so that you might understand the emphasis of the thing. But anyway, ever since then it's been one long round of conferences and international travel, riding on the back of the work of his researchers and taking protracted amounts of study leave. So that he can study his herbaceous border more like. Reading his work is the academic equivalent of watching the Rolling Stones at Wembley: tired, unoriginal and still banging out the same old tunes."

"Ah…" said Erica. "Very good."

"It's true. All true."

"And 'Clag Features'?" She asked slowly, her lips pursed expectantly.

"Oh it's the hygiene thing again." Said Carmi dismissively. "Some days he has these vile lumps of eye cheese that just sit in the corner of his eyes all morning. It's disgusting. He's a clag monster. I can't bear to look at him sometimes I swear.

"And he's so fundamentally inappropriate too." Carmi went on. "He addressed a meeting of the department administrators last week to discuss new support arrangements and in his opening line he included the word 'peripatetic'. Honestly. You could see all these people glazing over, hoping that someone else was taking notes or could translate."

Erica, not entirely sure of the meaning of 'peripatetic' herself, said simply and quietly, "Oh".

A cool gust of wind embraced them as they headed away from the central university buildings towards the Pavilion. A fine spray of rain touched their cheeks and a handful of leaves skittered along the edge of the path as if accompanying their progress.

"*Jesus*. So much for an Indian summer." Said Carmi, pulling Erica closer to her side.

The banter that they shared was the antidote to the working day. It was a private to-ing and fro-ing that they both treasured. Duncan and Erica had achieved something similar when they were first courting. With a diminishing closeness however had gone their private jocularity, extinguished by degrees by Duncan's self indulgent diatribes and Erica's subsequent agitation.

They pushed open the heavy glass door of the Pavilion bar and took a flutter of leaves in with them as they entered. A plate of chips and a couple of glasses of tomato juice were ordered hastily from an agitated barman struggling to cope with the lunchtime rush. They sat side by side in a high-backed corner seat and watched a stream of students and staff come and go, filling the tables and lining the bar of the small eatery outpost. Sports plaques and faded photographs of cricket teams covered the walls and Erica and Carmi were content to sit awhile in silence listening to the steady chatter. The arrival of their food snapped them back into the focus of their own company and Carmi set about ripping open sachets of tomato sauce and vinegar.

"God these smell good." She said inhaling the oily steam. "Should've ordered two bowls."

Erica watched her friend dig in for a few moments weighing up the impact of the chips on her own figure, at once resolving to allow Carmi to eat more than her fair share.

"I'm still waiting." Said Carmi, her mouth full.

Erica took a delicate bite out of a long hand-cut chip and sat back against the worn leather seat.

"It's the new lodger." She said. "I met her last night and well, dad was beside himself, all over her, like a dog on heat."

"Excellent. About bloody time."

Erica screwed up her face in the fearlessly over-animated manner of the young, whose skin is still tight elastic.

"Oh come on Erica. He deserves a bit of excitement. He's been dead from the waist down for a decade at least. Surely."

Carmi had stepped over a line and Erica sipped quietly from her drink in an unequivocal recognition of this.

"I was just teasing." Carmi said, her head lowered and eyes wide. "What did she look like?"

"Well, a bit bizarre really. Quite tall, enough foundation to sink a ship, *blue* mascara, and she was wearing knee-length khaki shorts with *heels*. Tasteless in my view."

Carmi nodded her head from side to side in a manner of weighing up this description. Shorts with heels was evidently off Erica's fashion radar, but lingering near the centre for Carmi if you had the legs to pull it off.

"She had quite nice hair actually – a thick blond bob – very French. But she had this lip liner – honestly Carmi you should have seen it – she could've passed for a transvestite. Oh and she had perfectly manicured nails and wore lots and lots of perfume – the really ancient stuff from the Seventies that smells like grannies."

Carmi screwed up her face. "Ooh."

Erica went on. "You get the picture. Says she's in need of somewhere for a few months or a year which, reading between the lines means that she's either just changed job or she's split up from somebody. Anyway, she was flirting with dad, sort of, teasing him. Giggling in this high voice that was *so* false."

"How old?"

"Dunno. Well about fifty, maybe younger. Younger than dad by a mile that's for sure. Oh and the worst part, she had one of those limp hand shakes that makes you despair when you receive it off another woman. I mean if you're gonna shake hands, shake hands, don't just offer up the end of your limb for mild agitation. I think it's rude, I think it's like saying 'I think you could be infectious and I don't want to touch you'."

"Jes*us*." Said Carmi leaning against the back of the seat with Erica. "You really didn't like this woman did you?"

"Well I didn't say that. She just seems false." Erica paused to give a formal wave of acknowledgement to a colleague across the room. She exhaled heavily and folded her arms. "I suppose it's just that dad agreed she could move in without asking me. He was even saying to her that there was no need to bother with a contract, all dismissive and over-the-top friendly, even though we *agreed* that we'd have a contract no matter who. I even went out and bought one of those legal packs last week. You know, a do-it-yourself landlady in a box type thing."

Carmi nodded. "So when's she moving in?"

"Not sure, could be next week." Erica stretched her legs out under the table deciding that listening to herself was uncomfortable – she was hearing a dislikeable over-reaction to a relatively unremarkable situation. It seemed easier to change the subject than to justify her comments.

"So anyway, I came in this morning and Anita's on to me like a rash enquiring after my wellbeing. It's as if she *knows*. It's 'how's your dad these days, how's the house, are you OK in Brenly with all these burglaries?' etcetera. And I'm like 'Fine thanks. I've got some budgets to look over and report to finish for the Dean by lunchtime in case you didn't know.' Well you know what I mean – I didn't *actually* say that."

Carmi raised her eyebrows.

"She's weird." Erica went on. "I swear sometimes she says things about stuff that I've never told her."

"Like what?"

"Like the other day she said something about dad being near retirement and what were his plans. Not only is that none of her business but how does she know dad's thinking of retiring?"

"Well I guess she must know he's in his late fifties or thereabouts. Not sure. Guesswork?"

"Yeah, but why should she care? Oh I dunno."

"She is a little…." Carmi paused and looked up at the ceiling. "*Challenging* sometimes. But fundamentally she's pretty sweet. Scatty, but well meaning."

"I know, I know. It's just the whole over-the-top compensatory motherly thing that bothers me. Work is work, home is home and somehow Anita wants to mix them up, because she wants us to be pals and I'm not sure why. She's not like that with anybody else."

"Believe me honey, thank your lucky stars you're not working for Clag Features."

Erica smiled. "So *then*, Duncan comes up looking terrible and asking for some painkillers. Says he thinks he's got a temperature and – get this – hasn't felt so tired since he stayed up all night listening to the results of the general election."

Carmi grunted. "The man's a hedonist."

"I felt so sorry for him. I just wanted to give him a hug, take care of him you know? But it was a good feeling – well for me it was – like I'd arrived at a point where I actually felt something for him that was totally different from before. Like *platonic* was suddenly very comfortable."

"Oh right." Said Carmi encouragingly. "And did you tell him that?"

"Of course not. I gave him some paracetamol and told him to go home." Erica picked at the remaining chips. "I might even ring him later to see how he is."

The sound of people talking in the bar had reached a point where it was no longer possible to speak in a normal voice and be heard. Standing space was all that remained and students waded their way to their friends holding up clutches of drinks at head height. A table of a dozen or so middle aged men, bearded and wearing fleece jackets and walking boots, dominated the seating area, one frail-looking female among them in matching attire. A younger man, sporting a more kempt goatee politely removed the last remaining stool that had been at Erica and Carmi's table, and joined the group.

"Geologists." Noted Carmi sucking tomato juice from ice cubes that blocked its path in the glass.

Erica nodded in agreement. "Mmm."

"The new Ph.D students at the end – farthest away – you must recognise them. They've moved in to the floor beneath you. They've got beards now too. Perhaps they only let you join the department as a post grad if you're prepared to grow your facial hair."

Erica nodded again. "It's true. It's part of the application. And our other friend?" She asked flicking her eyes briefly to the young woman amongst them. "What of her criteria?"

"Armpit hair." Said Carmi matter of factly. "It's the Jackson Five under there I'm sure."

Erica laughed into her drink, a brief convulsion bringing up an ice cube that plopped back into her glass. Drops of tomato juice sprayed her face and it was Carmi's turn to laugh in a deep bellow that carried above the sound of the voices.

She went on. "And what's with the outdoor gear? Did it require an expedition to reach the Pavilion? Why do you need walking shoes for the office and trousers with loops for your caribenas in order to get to work? Save it for the fieldwork guys *puh*lease."

"It's the rule of the geologist. A bit like Scouts – be prepared."

Carmi sat up straight and made a cone with her hand against her mouth. "Be prepared for a sudden and unexpected change in dimension." She said affecting the voice of an announcement-maker. "Remain calm. Your office will shortly turn into a shale field and you may be required to spend several hours participating in a treacherous expedition through a late Pleistocene lava forest. Basic hiking gear is a must."

The man that had taken the stool from them had been sitting with his back to Carmi and Erica. He turned around and delivered a warm grin, his cheeks pushed high up his face, forcing a squint.

"Oh sorry!" Whispered Carmi, putting her hand to her mouth. The man shook his head, still smiling, and returned to face his colleagues.

"Jesus. I really ought to keep my voice down."

"Ah… definitely not." Erica said and rubbed the palm of her hand against Carmi's shoulder. "Definitely not." She paused. "But anyway, he's yummy."

"Listen to you. Can't keep your eyes off the men. Which reminds me, have you heard from the Irish one – the policeman?"

"A bit. We're in touch but he's sort of busy with holidays and work. We've got a date pencilled in for the end of next week."

"Blimey. At this rate you'll be holding hands by Christmas."

Erica shifted in her seat uncomfortably now keen to leave the noisy bar. She wasn't certain herself of the ways things might progress with Connor and was profoundly unsure of how to tackle their next meeting.

"C'mon let's go. I'm seeing someone at two and I'm not prepared. I ought to be getting back."

They shuffled out slowly, through the crowded tables and turned back at the door to look at the young man that had smiled at them. From his seat he raised his glass and they fell out in to the bluster of the afternoon giggling and stumbling as if themselves, inebriated.

They marched quickly back towards the main university buildings. The wind was against them, and then for them, and then against them again, pushing them along and holding them back. When they reached the point of departure outside the Earth Sciences building they were warmed from the walk, Erica with blushed cheeks.

"I won't be around next week." Said Carmi in the manner of announcing an afterthought. "I'm going to Jamaica with mum."

Erica was taken aback and frowned. "What? Why?"

"Hortense died on Sunday – my grandmother – so I'm to go to the funeral." Carmi stabbed the heel of her shoe into a gap in the path and looked down. "It's OK. I never liked her. Only met her once when I was a kid – she came over for a funeral – but even then before I knew the facts, I never liked her."

"Oh." Said Erica, frowning. The fact that Carmi was about to undertake some serious travel – it would appear for the first time in her life – was unexpected news.

"She sent mum over here in the Fifties to stay with her sister – my aunt. Mum was ten at the time. She said that she'd be over to join her. But she never came. She chose to stay with her son – my Uncle Simon." Carmi looked up into Erica's face. "Who, ironically, never cared that much for Hortense and buggered off to America as soon as he was old enough." Carmi sighed and continued as if wrapping up a story that was a tedious exercise to her. "So mum's got all these unanswered questions like: why didn't you want me? Why did you send me away? What did I do wrong? Etcetera. And she'll never have any answers. Hortense went a bit doolally at the end anyway and was never one for making a lot of sense apparently. So I don't know that mum would have got the answers she was looking for."

"Wow." Said Erica, the chill in the wind finding its way up her coat sleeves. It seemed like a highly unsatisfactory ending to a painful family tale.

"So you're going to give your mum some support?"

"Yeah, plus I want to see Uncle Simon – he's fab – and all the others. Reckon it'll be a bit of a knees up." Carmi scratched her head. "I'm not sure." She paused. "It has the potential to be very very strange or really quite interesting and fun. If that's possible – for a funeral I mean."

They had spent an hour together and Carmi had not mentioned the trip once. It was the kind of thing that Erica recognised in herself. When she had a 'should I, shouldn't I?' decision to make, the answer often came to her via a revelation to someone else. It would pop up in conversation, as the right thing to do became apparent. Perhaps Carmi had been wondering whether to go to the funeral and had in that instant, made up her mind.

"I'm sure they'll make a big fuss of you." Said Erica and pulled her in for a hug.

"Yeah, yeah, it'll be fine. I'll see you when I get back. Obviously."

"Obviously."

"OK mate, take care – "

"Oh there was one more thing." Said Erica. "I'm going to be ordering some more stuff off the Internet. Like last time. Is it OK if I have it sent to your address again?"

Carmi smiled with half her mouth. "Yeah, 'course. As long as you're not going to get me into trouble."

"No, no. Nothing like that." Said Erica, her guts shifting unpleasantly.

They bade their farewells and Carmi clipped down the path towards her office, sturdy and direct. Erica looked back at her retreating form and headed inside.

FOURTEEN

For some time, Duncan had kept a diary of sorts. It acted as a prompt when recalling recent events for his mother the phone each week. He would prepare by having an accurate picture of an evening's television schedule so as he didn't interrupt her viewing of *Antiques Roadshow* or the latest costume drama. He would also take notes as his mother talked, jotting down some of the more important events that moved her world, so that he could refer back to them when they next spoke, check on progress and be assured that difficulties were ironed out. It was rudimentary mastery over an inherited lack of short term memory that doubled as an aid to composing the Christmas family newsletter. His mother would post photographs and headline events that she wanted captured and Duncan would compose a two-columned pastiche of his and his mother's lives, and send it out to relatives in Poland. He kept the composition to two sides of A4: one side in English and the other in Polish and poured over dictionaries and Internet translation pages to check over his work.

There hadn't been much worth saying since Barcelona. The entries had been kept short and factual and he had declined from speaking to his mother for two weeks initially feigning a need to be required for extra shifts. By late summer though, a new routine had emerged to his free time and the urge for that extra bounce in his step at the glorious start of the autumn had gone unsuppressed.

Dealing with a heavy cold therefore, was frankly unfair given that things were beginning to jog along with a new rhythm. It was a tedious and lonely affair and Duncan sat on the sofa in his flat flicking through his diary and making a single, lame entry for the week.

Heavy cold. Took first afternoon off sick in two years.

That was all. Hardly an entry worth recalling for the Christmas newsletter. He clicked the biro nib in and out repeatedly with his thumb and watched a cartoon on the television, the sound muted. He had brought the chaos of his bedroom into the lounge: the sacred, untouched space that was kept clear by mutual agreement. His flat mate had latterly retreated into his own room, such was his aversion to it. Duncan knew he had driven his friend away and felt all the more miserable for it, partly in irritation that Andy couldn't just lighten up for five minutes, and partly because he felt too wretched to do anything about it.

He flicked back a few pages in his diary.

Been trawling web stats at work – boring. New manager's got an obsession with meddling. Wants me to weed out the time wasters and find out who's been doing the most surfing. Not cool. Found something interesting though – looks like E's been searching for drugs for testicular cancer. Hope Harry's OK.

He shut the notebook and blew mightily into a handkerchief, throwing it onto the floor afterwards to sit amongst others of its kind, alongside used plates and a couple of half empty mugs. His throat was dry and he coughed feebly a few times for effect even though there was no one about to hear him.

The flat was too warm for September. Duncan had put the heating on when he'd got home but sat about in a shabby short-sleeved t-shirt and his standard work chinos, both sweating and shivering intermittently, the stench of his breath casting a stale odour over the whole flat. He rested his head fully back on the sofa and stared at the ceiling, his body leaden and his motivation to move, zero.

The phone rang out a couple of times and he lurched pathetically to answer it.

"Haddo." He said, emphasising the stuffiness in his nasal passages in case he was answering to someone from work.

"Oh hi D, it's me."

He said nothing.

"Erica."

He paused. "Yeah."

"Umm. Just wondered how you were doing."

"Crap." Said Duncan flatly and then broke into a protracted, half-forced coughing fit which he quickly regretted.

"Oh D, you poor thing." Said Erica. "Is Andy back from work yet?"

"No." Duncan let the word hang, offering no elaboration on the matter. He suspected that Erica was at once thinking that she ought to offer to come over and then as quickly, finding a reason not to.

"Oh right." She said. "I'm sure he'll be home soon. If he doesn't and you need me at all, just let me know."

"He's pissed off with me I think. Doesn't like being around sick people."

"You mean that the place is a tip?" Offered Erica gently.

Duncan sniffed. "Yeah."

"You'd think he'd chill out a bit when his best mate is poorly. Honestly, I don't know why he's so uptight."

Duncan was amused by Erica's assessment of his flatmate's reaction to his illness. All the time they had been together, Andy could never have put a foot wrong, always the golden boy, the example-setter. Perversely, now that there was no need to make comparisons between them, no need to pursue attempts to improve Duncan in some way, Erica chose to side with Duncan in matters of general reasonableness.

He reached into a box of tissues, extracted two and stuffed one up each nostril with his forefinger. "How's your dad?" He asked, the tissues flapping about on his face.

"He's fine. You know, working hard. Why?"

"Just wondered."

"We're getting a lodger. Probably this French woman that he interviewed last night. He seems quite keen on her. She's put a spring in his step anyway."

Duncan fiddled with the protruding ends of the tissues.

"How's your mum?" Asked Erica.

"Fine thanks."

Duncan moved pendulously between the agitation he really ought to feel for the false sympathies coming from his ex girlfriend and being mildly excited to be hearing from her during a time of need.

"Sorry Erica. I'm not feeling very chatty. You do the talking. What have you been up to?"

"Oh this and that. Nothing much really. Just a bit of decorating, helping dad out at work…"

Erica continued, passing comment on the minutae of working life and then more excitedly, the news of Carmi's sudden trip to Jamaica. Duncan grunted at intervals and flicked silently between TV stations. He settled on a channel that was showing re-runs of *Friends* and thought briefly of how young the actors all looked.

Erica finished, a vague buzz in his ear. "…And that's about it really."

"It was the blond one that you used to like wasn't it?" Asked Duncan. "The one who married Brad Pitt."

"What?"

"In *Friends*."

"Jennifer Anniston. Yeah." There was a pause. "You're watching telly."

Duncan pulled one of the tissues out from his nose and inspected its dampness.

"I'm gonna go now. Clear up before Andy gets back."

"Oh right. OK." Said Erica, an unequivocally disappointed edge to her voice.

"Call the search party if I'm not back in a couple of days." He tried to say as cheerfully as possible to elicit a sub text of an apology for cutting Erica short.

After half an episode of *Friends*, which didn't so much as raise a glimmer of mirth within him, he reached for his diary and wrote messily.

Spoke to Erica properly, first time in ages. She didn't mention that bloke. Harry's OK though.

Duncan surveyed the mess about him. He flung his diary, Frisbee-like, onto the floor and fell back into the sofa.

The first week of Monique settling in to the Old Rectory were like the visits from foreign students who used to come and stay in the summer months when Erica was a teenager. Harry had gone through a phase of bringing pupils from the local language school under the roof to ease the blow of paying for Janice's wedding. There had been weeklong bursts of animated hospitality and a polite to-ing and fro-ing in the kitchen at 7am that had tested Erica's patience at a time when she was not suited to geniality.

The fridge had been well-stocked, surfaces wiped and polished clean and bins emptied before they were full. It had been a curious but overall positive respite from the normal routine, and one that had been made all the more bearable by the fact that it was for a known period of time, that the restoration of their quiet regime was imminent.

Now, the house was pulsing somehow from the overspill of Monique's presence: shoes – endless pairs of shoes in the hallway – magazines and half finished drinks in the lounge. There was classical music in the morning seeping up the stairs long before Erica was due to rise, and more beefy Latin rhythms to greet her when she arrived home from work. There was a hubbub about the place at the beginning and end of the day: the phone rang more often, calls from family and friends in France; the suck of cork from wine bottles and the earthy chink of glasses on stone replaced the whistle of the old steel kettle after sunset. There were tall fluffy loaves in the bread bin, yoghurts and fruit in abundance and a line of fresh herbs in flimsy plastic pots on the kitchen windowsill. The smell of brewing coffee permeated the wood of the house drifting into Harry's dreams in the morning, and the hallway held the residue of Monique's perfume, rigorously applied morning and evening.

Erica moved politely around her new lodger assuming that the light touch of chaos that she had brought in to the house was either a settling in period or the expression of relief of having left some oppressive former life. Erica took to eating breakfast at work and lingered at her desk at the end of the day for longer than necessary. It wasn't that she disliked Monique per se, it was more the sense of change that she had brought to the house and the lives of her and Harry. She lingered over whether this flippant decision to bring in a lodger might somehow have changed the course of their lives permanently and without warning: had she moved too swiftly to fix things and instead had altered the one enduring comfort in her life?

Finding solace in the garden was increasingly off the agenda too aside a couple of glorious afternoons sweeping up leaves with Harry and preparing the garden for winter. They had lit bonfires that had seen Erica mesmerised; staring at the leafy orange fragments pouring into the sky was a therapy for any malady in her books. Drinking the odour of wood smoke from the collar of her coat after the event was a coming home smell, drenched in childhood, satisfying and crushed in an instant by Monique's next line of questioning.

"What is the red tree called? It is as if it was yellow only this morning and red by this evening. A quick flush."

"It's an Acer." Erica had said, met with a blank face. "A maple. We planted it after a storm a few years ago."

"Oh you know so much about the garden. When did this interest start?"

And so on. There didn't seem to be any discernable pause for breath. It was a job to edge past her and slip up the stairs to her bedroom without scrutiny – the first floor at least was not included in Monique's rented space. Erica found herself spending more time there, borrowing a small TV from Carmi and settling down in Ellen's old room amid worn cushions and throws, making tea from an electric kettle and reading battered second-hand novels long into the evening.

To add to the frustration was the endless complication of Connor's schedule. His shift work meant that by the time they had found a date that was mutually agreeable to meet up again, well over a month had passed and Erica was rather less excited by the prospect of seeing him. It had occurred to her that he could even be stalling things altogether until a note arrived one day on the doorstep attached to a small bouquet of freesias. It had read simply:

To Erica. Thinking of you. Connor.

The only other time someone had bought her flowers was Duncan who had got the date wrong for St Valentine's (the 13th February and a Friday no less) and delivered pale orange lilies to her office prompting a bout of hysterics from Carmi and some gentle questioning from Professor Singh. The lilies had been placed in a clinical glass jug and left in Erica's office over the weekend.

The freesias, however, were more celebrated: they were placed on the shrine that was Erica's large bedside cabinet, hidden from view in her own private territory.

When Erica did eventually meet Connor again, it was her turn to bear gifts. They met in a Japanese restaurant in the city centre, fast and funky and serving over-salted food. Erica had awkwardly placed a large pot of homemade jam on the table between them seconds after her arrival. Connor, grateful but unable to fit the jar into any of his pockets and equally amused by this fact, had put it back on the table where it stood, rosy and homemade next to contemporary steel salt and soy sauce dispensers until Erica, overcome with embarrassment, put it back into her bag.

The restaurant was laid out with long wooden tables and benches, upmarket canteen style, the clientele discouraged from lingering by fast service and an open plan kitchen that clattered and sizzled over the table talk. They ordered the same dishes from the menu and struggled with chopsticks, emerging onto the street, full and thirsty after only an hour.

For mid October it was mild but still blustery and the impending clock change had brought out winter coats and scarves from dusty hibernation. Erica and Connor strolled to a nearby pub in the darker backstreets and picked up where they had left off.

"Don't forget to give me the jam later." Said Connor arching his spine against a tall, wooden seat.

"Oh yes." Erica looked into her gin and tonic. "I picked them myself – the blackberries. Well, with my sister and the twins. I wouldn't go blackberry picking alone."

"No." Said Connor, deep voiced, agreeing. "Not round your way at least. Nowhere's safe."

"It's a shame when you can't even step outside your own door to pick some blackberries and not feel safe. Well…" Said Erica tailing off in thought, "Monique would I'm sure. She's always off strolling about, usually after work. And I don't mean down to the corner shop and back. She walked all the way cross country to a pub last weekend, on her own, clutching my Ordinance Survey map and wearing one of dad's old wax jackets, which is now marinated in eau do cologne." Erica pursed her lips.

"Yves Saint Laurent all-weather gear."

"Something like that. Probably had all the foxes in a ten-mile radius running for cover." Erica paused, wary of slipping into another cynical assessment of Monique but sensing that Connor was enjoying it. "For a teacher she doesn't seem to know very much, and she doesn't seem to spend very much time teaching."

"Maybe she just does enough to get by."

"Yeah, but my old friends that are teachers now are all rushed off their feet and are always – and I mean *always* – banging on about how tired they are."

Connor took a sip of his beer. "Maybe she's not a very good teacher."

"You'll have to meet her." Blurted out Erica, grappling at once with having invited Connor to the Old Rectory so inexactly and wondering if in fact Monique might be his type.

Connor said nothing for a while but smiled warmly across the table at Erica.

"That'd be good. I could check her out, see if she really is after your dad. I'm pretty good at reading the whole body language thing."

Erica thought that Connor could actually be quite expert in deciphering body language given his profession. She scratched her head and considered that touching certain parts of your body during speech could indicate honesty or conversely, a lack of integrity. She watched Connor smile more broadly, cheekily even, scratched her nose, forehead and then twisted her forearms around each other, placing her chin on an upturned palm.

"Very good, very good." Said Connor laughing. "The crossing of the forearms indicates a highly disingenuous character, very likely given to poisoning jam and distributing it to unsuspecting males in order to extract the truth from them."

Erica felt a loaded blush rise up from her neck. She coughed into her hand and laughed falsely, reeling from the horrible collision of a growing affection and her own duplicity. Testing her ability for Carmi-style extroversion didn't seem so appropriate any more.

It was time to crack on to other subjects. She had listened with interest that evening to Connor's stories, what he had been up to since they had last seen each other, more on his family, and had had struggled to match his litany of activities. The atmosphere was easy, positive: shared interest to an extent but enough diversity to keep intrigue fresh. Despite her earlier paranoia-induced wobbliness, she wanted to press on, get the questions over with so they could get back to the good stuff.

"So, can I ask you some questions for my research?" Erica was pushed from behind and lurched into the table. It was an accident, a drunk student on a meander back from the bar. Connor scowled at him and seemed to Erica to puff up for a moment.

"I don't know. Things are so much more civilised when the students have gone home." Mused Connor.

"Really? I mean crime wise – statistically?"

"Oh no. I dunno. A little maybe. I just mean out and about, the pubs, you know."

"Yeah yeah sure." Erica's voice was squeaky, a bubble caught in her throat. She pulled a notebook from her bag and placed it gingerly on to the sticky table.

"But yeah, fire away." Said Connor nodding towards the book.

"I just wanted to know if there'd been a drop in crime since we last met, just Oxfordshire that is, this month. And just general crime, well, violent crime. The stuff I asked you about over the phone."

Connor leant back and immediately leant forward again. "Jesus these seats are hard. It might be the quaintest pub in town but you'd have thought they'd have replaced the Mediaeval seating by now."

Erica tried to laugh sweetly but accidentally elicited a snort instead.

Connor pretended not to notice.

"Well I haven't brought anything with me." He said raising his hands. "I did ask, plus I got a comparison with the neighbouring counties, but nothing to report in terms of variation from the seasonal average. And the specific villages you mentioned – presumably near pylons?"

Erica nodded affirmatively.

"Well there's nothing of statistical significance to report in those areas either. What I can do though is get some figures for you for September and then late October, something printed up so you can do your own comparisons. Do whatever you need to do with the data."

"Graphs." Erica smiled and slid her notebook on to her lap. "Yes, that would be good. End of October, in fact end of every month would be most helpful."

"No problem. But in terms of headline figures, no significant change." He paused. "Are you ever going to write anything in that notebook of yours?"

Erica slid the notebook into her bag and laughed feebly. "Yeah."

"So that's sorted. Good." Connor clapped his hands and rubbed them together. "So you'll have a drink with me next week then before I head to New York."

"New York?"

"Yup. I'm doing the New York marathon. Got a place last minute with a charity. Great excuse to stay with my cousin too. In fact, maybe you can take me out training at the weekend – you do the cycling, I'll do the running. I need to get some long runs in if I'm to get a half decent time."

FIFTEEN

Erica had had a restless night. The information from Connor that there was no difference in crime levels since the brewery contamination was bothersome. She worked late the following day, closing the door to her office to spend time on the Internet in private.

She considered the possibilities. The effect of the drug could have been too slow to have made an impact yet the literature suggested a very short period of time before testosterone levels dropped. Alternatively, the beer may not have reached its intended audience. She knew of the chain of pubs that ordered the brew she had contaminated and they were regular; supplies were fresh which was part of the success of the drink. Finally, the efficacy of the drug may have been destroyed by the brewing process itself: the boiling in the huge kettles may have affected things. It seemed to be the most likely explanation but left Erica frustrated at not having considered this possibility before. She searched a few other manufacturers in Asia that also produced drugs for testicular cancer to check prices, planning to order a greater quantity than before but to add it later in the brew. The logistics of this were not yet clear to her: when should she now add the powder? How could she avoid being seen meddling at a later stage of the brew when there could be brewers in attendance? More importantly, how could she guarantee that the powder would dissolve? She would need *some* heat for this to happen, just not a hundred degrees of it.

An hour later, hungry and hunched at her computer, rough sketches and notes strewn on scrap paper, she stared at the screen. Rubbing her forehead she pulled herself up to stretch and flicked back to some previous searches. Erica noticed material listed that she had not seen before, discussing the availability of the different drug manufacturers plus a frank document on a cancer charity's website that explained courses of treatment. It stated clearly that it was administered in the UK in liquid form via injection.

"Bingo."

She slumped down heavily on her desk at once thinking through the possibilities of pouring a liquid directly into the beer before it was bottled or barrelled, removing any need for dissolution – assuming that it didn't taste completely foul. A further hour later and Erica had found a distributor in Hong Kong prepared to sell her a few hundred vials at no insignificant cost. Erica split the order between herself and Carmi using her home address and Carmi's work address for delivery, unsure of what Customs would make of it. With Carmi's credentials and the University's postal address as recipient, she was confident that at least one of the orders would get through.

From the brink of giving up on her scheme, Erica was once again immersed in it, up to her neck and yet only vaguely grappling with the gravity and invidiousness of her plan.

Harry – eyes fixed, foot tapping absently to music – was contemplating the finishing touches to his latest still life when the phone rang. It made him jump in his seat but was not sufficient to rouse him to answer it. He wanted instead to decide there and then whether to add the dab of red paint that was hanging on the end of his brush or to leave the painting as it was and not meddle with it any further. It was a small oil – one that he thought he could get away with hanging in the hallway without too much resistance from Erica – the subject matter fitting for the season: a small harvest of rowan berries, rosehips and chestnuts arranged on a rumpled table cloth. The arrangement he painted from was set by the window for best lighting and had decayed only fractionally over a period of weeks.

Eyes still fixed on the canvas, he stepped slowly back towards the door to listen to the answer machine downstairs that clicked into life to play Erica's polite greeting.

Janice's voice, amplified by the fact that she was shouting into her mobile phone, echoed up the stairs.

"Ooh." Said Harry quickly and ran into his bedroom to pick up another receiver.

"Hi, hello, Janice, yes I'm here." Said Harry, panting a little.

"Hi." I was just returning your call. It's taken a while I know." Janice's voice was breathy, set to the backdrop of what could only have been an urban street.

"You're in town." Said Harry.

"Yup."

"I'm off today too. Well I mean I'm at home – I've got to work on Saturday so I'm having my weekend now." Said Harry, upbeat. "What are you up to?"

"I'm in town. What did you call for at the weekend? Anything urgent?"

"No, just to say that Monique's living here now and we'll be collecting rent off her next week. So, I just wanted to know what arrangements we needed to make about sending the money on to you. Thought we could maybe just ask her to pay directly into your account."

Harry listened to the sound of fading police sirens and people's voices through the receiver.

"Hello?" He asked.

"Yes, I'm here."

"OK, well, I just said –"

"Yes I heard you. Look don't worry, you keep the money." Said Janice her voice tired, resigned. "I can't take it off you. It'd be like payment for a debt – one that you'd never be able to pay back anyway."

"Janice!"

"I'm serious dad. Keep it. You and Erica enjoy it."

"But I thought that the boys started at the new school last month."

"They've started at the one they were originally going to go to. No fees. Keith was against it."

"Right." Said Harry balancing the paintbrush across the shade of his bedside lamp. "You mean Keith didn't want to be seen accepting charity."

"Something like that."

"Well take it anyway Janice. You don't need to tell him."

Harry heard the sound of a car door slam and the background noise extinguished. He was about to restate his suggestion when Janice spoke quietly.

"Are you suggesting that I hide something from my spouse?" Her voice was clear and caustic.

Harry wiped his forehead with his palm and sat down on his bed. "No love. Well. Yes. I mean, well maybe we could put it towards something for the boys, or towards a holiday or something, for all of us. I dunno. I'm just thinking out loud here.

"Nothing devious." He added. "I just thought that you needed the money which is why we went through this whole rigmarole of getting a lodger in the first place."

"No dad, it was a kind suggestion by my little sister to make up for the fact that you won't do what is just and reasonable and what you owe us."

Harry put his head in his free hand, bending down to stare at the floor. "I'm not selling the house for as long as Erica is happy here. I told you that in the summer."

"And I'm *so* not going to have this discussion with you again dad. Just do us all a favour and do the decent thing for once in your life. And anyway, I hear you get on rather well with the French woman. You always were attracted to the foreign ones."

"Ellen!"

"It's Janice actually. And I've got to go and pick the boys up from school now."

"Janice I mean –" He heard the sound of the car engine starting up and the phone clicked dead. He remained still.

"Um, uh, hi."

Harry looked up. Monique was standing in the bedroom doorway clutching a cup of tea.

"I brought this up." She held the mug out towards him. "Um, the uh, the answer machine was playing in the hall." Her voice was one of quiet anxiety.

"Oh god, I'm sorry." Said Harry and stood up, placing the phone back on the hook. He took the mug from Monique. "Thanks."

"That's OK."

"And sorry. You shouldn't have heard that. I didn't think you were in."

"I just got back from school."

"Right."

They were awkward, strangers again, Monique taking the opportunity to brazenly eye up a room she was not acquainted with.

"I'm making coffee." She pointed vaguely towards the stairs and backed gingerly onto the landing.

Despite the preoccupation of the row with Janice fresh in his mind, Harry could read Monique's body language. "You want to have a look about up here?"

"Oh well, yes. If you don't mind. Thanks. I saw the paintbrush but I wasn't sure…"

"This way." Harry ushered Monique into his studio, formerly his and Dorothy's bedroom. There was a line of half-finished canvases leaning against one wall, several completed pieces propped loosely into mounts, and a small stereo on the stripped oak floor, paint-splattered and quietly beating out jazz in mono. The room was white, the plaster shabby in places and the only painting on the walls was a three foot square portrait of Dorothy set in an ornate oak frame. It faced the window, framed again by the last splutters of the late autumn sunset that edged through the window.

Monique stood near the door, hands clasped childishly, her eyes drawn at once to Dorothy's portrait and then to the easel that held Harry's latest work.

Harry put his tea on the floor and picked the still life up by its edges, hesitated for a moment and then set it back again.

"I'm not going to sell the house." He said solemnly. "Not just now, and not for a good while, so don't worry. And you're very welcome here."

Monique smiled, nodding politely. "That's good to know. Thank you. I like it here."

Harry bent down to collect his mug from the floor. "That coffee must be ready by now." He said and deftly ushered Monique out of the room and towards the stairs.

"Oh for god's sake!" Screeched Erica slamming on the car brakes. The subject of her anger – another driver meandering into the road in front of her – continued on at a speed that suggested that they were oblivious to other road users. Erica strained to see if she could make out the silhouette of an elderly person at the wheel and in so doing, find it in her heart to excuse them in some way.

It was Guy Fawkes night and she was heading cross-country to Janice's to have a bonfire with the boys in the garden. She had a packet of ten sparklers on the passenger seat and a bottle of ready-made mulled wine that rolled around the floor with each brake and turn. Her eyes drifted up to fireworks launched from back gardens and village greens against a clear and freezing night sky; she was steady in her thoughts and not lifted by the spectacle.

The build up had been unmissable: a steady increase in the release of explosives over the preceding weeks – whistling, screeching shocks that punctuated the chilly nights. It had brought her and Monique together in some small way in dealing with a terrorised stray cat one evening. They had coaxed it from the porch where it had become lodged between an enormous potted plant and a fallen shoe rack, the shared and unabashed concern for so delicate a creature creating a small bond between them, before returning again to their separate parts of the house.

November 5th was seized upon as extraordinary and exciting as a child and then considered wistfully as an adult. Erica, whilst frightened of fireworks when young, had observed her own attention turning in recent years to the ghastly and ever-more realistic Guys she had seen mounted on municipal bonfires. One had been so disturbing at an event staged by the district council the previous year that she had written to complain. Atop the mound of damaged wooden pallets and unwanted ply, had been placed effigies of Mr and Mrs Guy Fawkes sitting on a two-seater sofa in front of a small plastic table and portable television. When the fireworks display was over and the bonfire lit, she had refused to hoist either of the twins onto her shoulders to view the inferno, and had chastised Cleo for stopping to watch the flames rise up and consume the couple in the staged domestic furnace. Aside the obvious environmental issues with burning so much plastic and the curious addition of a *Mrs* Guy Fawkes to the equation, it was too grim to contemplate, made all the more sickening when the onlookers cheered with the crescendo of the flames. Celebrating a tradition was one thing, burning dummies of couples apparently relaxing in their own home was quite another.

It bothered Erica to consider this specific event as she drove, to have no apparent control over the recollection of this and other unsettling memories, some more recent than others. Remembering the alarming simplicity of contaminating a brew for a second time earlier in the week ebbed back and forth like a dark river through her conscience, nudging her into an increasingly black mood. Both of the shipments of drugs that she had bought had arrived from Hong Kong only a week after she had placed her order and she had intercepted them both before anyone else had had a chance to see them or to question her. She had spotted the one delivered to Carmi's office quite spectacularly on the day that her own parcel had arrived at home. The post trolley had been parked in her corridor, the delivery man making idle chat with a colleague in an adjacent room. Erica had sidled up to it, checked the names on the larger packages and deftly removed the delivery addressed to 'Dr Carmi Mills' from the pile, marching purposefully back to her office unseen.

The quantity had surprised her, insomuch as both parcels, whilst containing over a hundred vials between them, were only enough to fill two half-litre bottles. She had sweated in her bedroom that evening to extract the liquids, a chair pushed up against her door for fear of being disturbed, contented only by the knowledge that Harry would be working late. She had not trusted Monique to stay away, having previously observed the signature dents of her stilettos upstairs.

It had felt like an ugly activity, perverse even; not the decanting of the liquid per se, but making her way in secret over the various obstacles that could trip her up at any juncture. The only answers she had prepared were unconventional, political, based on apparently innocent assumptions that were never likely to hold any ground. Hence having to vocalise these answers was not an option. To Erica, there were only two possible outcomes that she had to contend with: the drug had a positive effect, or the drug had no effect at all. Other scenarios of being caught or causing harm were not to be entertained. The irony had not escaped her either, that it was precisely this mindset that drove the very group of men she abhorred to commit crime in the first place.

She had dealt with the ample polystyrene packaging by stuffing it into plastic sacks, launching them out of the tall sash window in her bedroom and calmly exiting the house, making a point of waving goodbye to Monique empty-handed as she left. From there she had collected them from the ground, driven to the outskirts of the city to buy a take-away, depositing the sacks en route in a large supermarket dustbin.

Having quickly established that the drug was relatively tasteless and had approximately the same viscosity as water, Erica had sampled (and duly spat out) a glass of beer containing several drops of it. There had been no discernable difference in the taste or texture of the beer and she had at once conceived her plan for the next contamination. Access to the brewing schedule would have been as easy as strolling into her father's office as she might have done any evening, but as it was, Harry had brought a copy home with him that week which he had poured over briefly and then abandoned on the kitchen table. Hawk-like, Erica had seized upon it, examined it for her own purposes and quickly ascertained that the next brew for the chain of local pubs that she had first targeted was taking place overnight on the following Monday. This brew would ferment for forty-eight hours and then be transferred to the holding tank for a further twenty-four before being put into barrels. Quite spectacularly, in Erica's view, the twenty four-hour period in which the beer was to be waiting idle in the holding tank there were no other brews scheduled. Despite the fact that two further brews would be simultaneously fermenting, there would be little else happening on the brewery floor aside normal cleaning activity, equipment maintenance and yeast checks. The filling of the barrels would take place for all three brews on the Thursday afternoon for dispatch the following morning. There had been therefore, an opening at a reasonable hour of the day, for Erica to pay a visit.

She had arrived late at the brewery after work on the Wednesday, timing her arrival so as not to bump into any of the office staff on their way home. Harry and two of the other brewers were in the floodlit yard, negotiating a mountain of pallets and barrels by forklift truck. The same young apprentice – Saul – that she had sent home the last time she had contaminated a brew, was cleaning around the yeast tanks. Most importantly, the offices were empty.

She had waved to Harry on her arrival in the car park and pointed up to the offices indicating that she'd wait for him there. Harry had held up the palms of his hands in response, his fingers outstretched, indicating that it would be ten minutes before he could join her. She had moved quickly into the offices and had made a swift assessment of the brewery from the viewing gallery: as scheduled, all four of the fermentation tanks had been in action, the holding tank was full and the rest of the brewery pristine, ready for the next day's brew. Aside the people she had already observed, no other staff were clocked on.

Erica had been wearing a small rucksack containing the decanted drug that sloshed and bumped about as she moved around the building. From Harry's desk she had looked over the security camera console to check that everything was as it had been minutes earlier on her arrival. With an easy flick of a switch, the cameras were idle and Erica had moved back onto the viewing gallery, rucksack hooked over her shoulder, her heart thumping. A ten-minute break in the CCTV footage would go unnoticed, and besides, the system reset itself every forty-eight hours.

The apprentice had had his head down, consumed by a wide, white dial in the yeast-culturing area, wiping around it, referring to a clip board tucked under his arm, and then back again. He did not even appear to acknowledge Erica as she had walked down the stairs and into the main brewing hall although she figured that he must have entered his peripheral vision. The hum of all of the fermentation tanks, their steady spew and trickle of foam, had covered the sound of her footsteps and Saul was out of sight in a few seconds.

The layout of the brewery was such that the holding tank sat alongside the main filling and bottling area by the entrance to the yard. A delivery of barley had been stacked ten pallets high, white sacks tight and dusty, mercifully obscuring the view of the yard from Erica's position.

The moments taken to contaminate the holding tank had been desperate. She had mounted a thin metal ladder welded to the side of the tank, considering that at any moment her father or any other of the brewers could have walked in from the yard, giving her only seconds to dismount. She had struggled with the bottles, her hands clammy and shaking and for a moment had lost her grip on one of the bottle tops, anxiously grappling with it to prevent it from falling. The simplicity of the task had become an exaggerated series of activities, fingers and brain marching to a different drum.

Having unplugged the main pipe into the tank, she had created her own dilemma of where to place the opened bottle. The roof of the tank was conical leaving no flat surface to rest it on. She had chosen to tuck it under her arm, conscious of a pain growing in her knees that were pushed against the sides of the ladder for balance. The absence of coordination was costing her heartbeats and she had become aware of a wetness around her toes, her feet mobile in her shoes, pressing on the thin rung of the ladder. The physical and moral discomfort of the act had claimed her senses and slowed the moment to make each breath an endurance.

Decanting the bottles had seemed to last an age and she had resealed the pipe and hopped off the ladder, moving swiftly across the floor, mounting the steps to the viewing gallery two at a time, her damp socks squeaking in her shoes. Sitting back at Harry's desk, she had been drawn to a digital clock flickering green on the television console: the whole exercise had taken only three minutes. Her heart had pounded, she had felt nauseous and light-headed at the sheer relief of it all being over. Everyone was where they had been when she had viewed them last over the cameras: a forklift truck moved slowly in monochrome from one side of the yard to the other and her father stood rubbing his hands against the cold.

Erica drove distractedly, staring half-focused on the taillights of the car in front, recalling the awful sickness she had felt sitting at Harry's desk earlier that week. It had been a simple enough plan to pull off but one that was inherently fraught with risk and relying heavily on good fortune and timing. What if this next contamination was successful? She could see no long term plan, no ongoing course of action that would build on these first efforts. The project, if it could be called such a thing, was neither scaleable nor sustainable. The future was a consideration Erica had not previously entertained in earnest and it cast a sense of futility over everything, one that suited her mood for a drive in the freezing cold of a November night to her sister's.

Janice was in full matriarch mode when Erica arrived, a wide plastic apron tied around her waist, directing Keith and Cleo in the kitchen to deal with baked potatoes and a large pan of chilli that simmered on the hob. She squeezed Erica bodily and immediately dispatched her into the garden to see if her guests would like more mulled wine.

There were six adults at the end of the garden, neighbours of Janice's that Erica had met on a few occasions, an awkward-looking girl of about seven or eight that appeared to be one of their children, plus Ellen. They stood roasting by an ample bonfire, Caspar and Benedict running in and out of view on the dark lawn as Erica made her way down. She smiled mischievously at the little girl, bade a polite *hello* to the other adults and strode up to Ellen.

"Helloooo." Said Ellen stepping forward to embrace her. "God you just get taller every time I see you."

Erica relaxed into her sister's arms, animatedly rocking her from side to side, a movement that eventually forced a protracted giggle as they fell apart from each other.

"Didn't know you were coming." Said Erica. "Where's your car?"

"Ah, long story. I came by train. Fran's got my car. She had to go and see her family suddenly." She waved her arms dismissively. "I'm staying over anyway." She reached into the pockets of a thick-knit knee-length cardigan and extracted a pouch of tobacco and some cigarette papers.

"You're smoking again."

"Don't." Ellen deftly rolled a knob of tobacco in her palm into a thin strip and placed it on a paper. "So. Any news? Tell me about the lodger. I hear she's a bit of a handful. German isn't she?"

"French. And yeah." Erica shuffled from one foot to the next, smiling, hands deep in her pockets. "She's OK. Didn't like her much at first but she's alright. Trying to pull off quirky, youthful fifty-something and instead looking like she's wearing her daughter's clothes. That kind of thing. Terrible taste in music and an insatiable addiction to coffee and wine. *And* being positioned next to the kitchen, kind of hard to ignore."

"Oh god. A bit intense then."

"Yeah, but dad likes her."

"So I've heard." Ellen licked the seam of the cigarette paper and put the thinnest end into her mouth. "He in the house?"

"No. He's not here. Well, he's working late and then he said he was going straight out for a drink. I don't think he realised Janice was having a – " Erica paused, lowering her voice "– party. In fact, I didn't know either. I just thought it was the five of us."

"Oh." She said.

"Well. Six. You never really know with Cleo. It being Saturday night."

Ellen lit the cigarette and held it out in front of her mouth to blow smoke over the end. "So, dad wasn't invited then?"

It wasn't so much a question as a statement and Erica raised her eyebrows.

"Bloody hell." Said Ellen. She opened her mouth to speak, a frown forming on her forehead, and then closed it, breaking into a wide smile at someone approaching from behind Erica. It was the little girl, wanting to know if she could have a stick like the twins had to poke at the fire. Ellen subtly flicked her cigarette into the flames and took her hand, ambling over towards a pile of fire wood and garden debris, straight into easy conversation. Children adored her, an intermediary between girl and big girl, someway past teenager, but not far enough to be ranked alongside parents. Erica though she should have been a teacher. She would have had entire classes wrapt and obedient where others had failed. Erica's own command of children was deeply insecure like she was unqualified in some way, made all the more nervous by the twins' unequivocal trust in her.

Ellen and the girl returned carrying between them a hefty log, and after a protracted *one-two-three* launched it haphazardly in to the bonfire. Instant consternation broke out amongst the adults at this inexpert attempt to stoke the flames, comprehensively ignored by Ellen who cheered and clapped with the girl at the flakes of burning debris that splayed out. Erica, deflecting their concern by collecting orders for a another round of drinks, headed back indignant at the approach Janice had taken to the evening. Her mood, fuelled jointly by her own misdemeanours and by her hormones, was dark enough to brave challenging Janice regarding Harry's absence.

Ellen, watching the back of her sister march purposefully across the lawn, now found herself jarred by an unshakeable feeling that tonight was the night that Erica might finally push the subject into irretrievable territory.

"I need four more mulled wines and a mug of hot Ribena." Said Erica thumping a handful of spent glasses onto the kitchen table. "And where's dad tonight?"

Cleo was holding out two plates for Janice to ladle chilli over huge baked potatoes. She seemed to shrink into a pair of oversized combats that appeared to consume the whole vision of her, and pulled the plates away too keenly, allowing some of the chilli to fall to the floor.

"I'll take these down." She mumbled and shuffled out of the back door.

Janice tore off an ample wad of kitchen roll. "Oh dear, look at this." She said.

"Didn't you invite him? You didn't did you?"

Keith swept the glasses from the table and busied himself with refilling them, his eyes down.

"Hey hey." Said Janice soothingly. "Let's not have a row please. We're just about to eat. We were going to have some fireworks first but I think I timed it all wrong. If I'd left the potatoes in any longer they would be powder by now and the chilli's hot enough to take the roof of your mouth off – as in temperature, not as in *hot* hot. The boys wouldn't like that."

She laughed needlessly, scooping chilli from the floor, but was the only one smiling.

"I don't want a row either Janice. I just want an answer. I can't bear arguing with you, but you need to understand that it's pretty difficult for me to make sense of this. I thought tonight was you, me, the twins and a bonfire for a couple of hours. How do you think I'm going to explain to dad that I saw not only you and the kids, but Ellen and Cleo as well? Plus a handful of friends, some of whom he actually knows."

"You don't have to explain anything." Said Janice, forcing a smile and moving to the sink to tackle a pile of crockery. "Now's not the time."

"Now's never the time." Tears backed up in Erica's eyes fury burning and convulsing in her belly. She was glowing, her coat still done up to the neck, beads of sweat tickling her back. "One woman out there – Suzie, the one with the little girl – she used to work in the office with dad, for about two years I reckon. Dad would love to have seen her, to say nothing of the boys and all of us."

Janice spun round, her smile now a tight line. "Yes but would they have wanted to see him?" She cocked her head.

Erica, jarred, opened her mouth to speak and instead allowed a stream of water to fall from her eyes.

"Oh poppet, no! I'm sorry. God I'm sorry." Said Janice at once, pulling off more of the kitchen roll and guiding Erica towards a chair. Keith shuffled past her towards the back door, glasses clanking on a metal tray.

"Keith honey, can you come back for the rest of the chilli?" Asked Janice urgently. "We'll need knives and forks as well."

Keith nodded and projected a half smile at Erica, who watched his altered form through a watery lens.

"What do you mean by that?" Continued Erica, full sobs emerging in waves. "Ellen wanted to see him. She thought he was coming."

She took hold of Erica's hand. "I just didn't think of it, I mean, I didn't think he'd like it."

"Bollocks." Said Erica, pulling her hand away. "What's it to be? You didn't think of asking him or you didn't think–"

"Oh I don't know." Said Janice, edgy again. "We can talk about it later."

"No!" Erica brought her fist down on to the table, unsettling a pile of stacked dinner plates. "Tell me now. Why don't you want him around? What's he ever done to you?"

"Nothing Erica. Nothing." Janice patted down the plastic apron that had formed into two large bulges on her lap and inhaled loudly. "It's what he did to mum."

The back door opened and Caspar and Benedict burst in, the young girl in tow, less shy now, part of the gang. They were breathless and stumbling over the doorstep, leaves stuck to their coats, hair awry, a sudden injection of neediness and joy that saw Erica hastily wipe the wetness off her face and onto her sleeve.

"Dad said we've got to get the rest of the chilli for everyone." Announced Caspar. "And some for us."

"Nice one Keith." Said Janice quietly and stood up to administer the food. "Erica could you get the knives and forks please?" She asked in a sing song voice betraying the atmosphere in the room.

Erica stared back at her sister, motionless, something unnerving to Janice, like fury, forming on her face.

The children were oblivious and worked in shifts to take the plates of food down to the end of the garden. Erica caught a glimpse of Ellen hovering by the back door but sat still, pulled down by a double dose of gravity, her mind blank, any remaining shred of optimism she had been holding for a positive outcome to the evening, obliterated by Janice's words.

SIXTEEN

The three shotguns that hung in the dining room had been reduced to one during the clearout preceding Monique's arrival. Harry had clung on to the only one that had ever been used in earnest – an early twentieth century hunting gun – and dispatched the others to a local auctioneer. He was reluctant to see it go although Erica had struggled to see the logic in keeping an heirloom of her mother's that she had had little interest in. They had arrived at a compromise, returning the ornately carved silver and walnut shotgun to its original leather case. It was locked away with a box of two-inch cartridges in the deep mahogany sideboard along with a mix of antique tat and ugly china figurines that had become a pain to get the duster around. Relics of the efforts of the nouveau riche – namely Dorothy's parents attempting to fill an ample home in the 1930s – the decent stuff had been siphoned off by Janice and Ellen over the years but no one had been interested in the guns.

    Erica was the only one to have had a practical brush with the gun, taking it, on Harry's advice, to the first Departmental Team Building Day at a grand hotel and conference centre in Buckinghamshire. A group forty-strong, of academics, technicians and administrative staff, were forcibly arranged into unlikely combinations and instructed to play giant Connect 4, build polystyrene rafts against the clock and shoot clay pigeons on a midsummer's day. Sidling up to the organisers, proudly clutching the polished double-barrelled antique, Erica had been swiftly taken aside by worried-looking staff and gently probed about licences and ammunition. She was lectured about how they couldn't possibly allow her to fire the gun on their premises and Erica had cursed her father for putting such a stupid idea into her head in the first place. As it was, she had been encouraged to stay behind at the end of the day by the principle clay pigeon shooter, who had extolled the world of vintage shotguns to her and promptly demonstrated how to load and fire the weapon. Erica had returned to work the following day with a bruised shoulder and the elevated status of having gone from the partially invisible graduate to borderline eccentric of the department.

The Old Rectory responded well to change. It embraced new inhabitants with a warmth that made you feel like you were visiting an old friend. It gave away secrets of itself little by little, the longer the acquaintance lasted. Its atmosphere was often commented upon, Harry throwing in his personal adage about the place: that it took a piece of the best of everybody that had ever lived there. This comment reduced any conversation held on the premises with him to an outpouring of sympathetic 'aahs' and 'yes of courses' and 'you must all miss her terribly' that grated on Erica and sent Janice into a tailspin.

For Erica, nowhere felt particularly comforting to spend any time alone in, aside possibly her bedroom. The Old Rectory was warm and familiar, it offered places to hide and whilst it was too isolated for Erica to feel truly at ease in the light of the burglaries, it generously exposed the movements of its occupants to anyone that could read it well enough.

By the time that she had abruptly returned home early from Janice's, two things were amiss: the hall was cold, despite the heating being on, as if someone had recently left a door open, and the kitchen door that was permanently propped open by a rusting antique iron, was closed.

A chill passed through Erica with a deeper penetration that any winter night could effect.

"Hello?" She said timidly, hovering by the front door. She felt in her pocket for her phone and walked back out of the house, got into the car and locked the doors. The house was still. The lamps set on timers were lit as they should be and a warm light spilled out of the house from windows on both floors. The end of the driveway was a good fifty feet behind her and Erica checked her rear view mirror, reassured by a steady trickle of car headlights in the road.

She dialled Connor without thinking and was put through to his voicemail after a protracted wait.

"Damn." She said, cursing that he was still in New York. She stared back at the house. Harry was out, mobile phone probably switched off; Monique was almost definitely out, god knows where and god knows for how long.

A firework from a garden some streets away whistled into the sky spilling red light onto the rumpled glass of the Rectory's front windows. Erica watched its reflection, glittering dashes of red, her fear cut in by a microsecond's contemplation of how time and gravity had rippled the antique glass.

"This is ridiculous."

She tried Harry's mobile and was redirected straight to his voicemail. She did not have Monique's number and instead called the house. The phone rang several times and Erica hung up at the sound of her own voice on the machine. She unlocked the car and gingerly made her way up to the house leaving the front door open as she entered.

The key to the sideboard was inexpertly hidden on the dining room door mantle and Erica made swift work of unlocking it and extracting the shotgun from its case.

Her mind was muddled. An abrupt exit from Janice's followed by a car journey spent chewing over the meaning of her sister's words had gnawed into her, new possibilities as to the family rift exposing themselves. Maybe Harry had had an affair. Or maybe Janice *thought* that he had had an affair. It seemed logical now and Erica was both annoyed at herself for not having pursued this line of thinking before and shattered at considering the possible truth of it. A person doesn't hold that level of resentment for their father for no reason at all, that much was obvious. Perhaps now that Erica was older, Janice thought she was able to deal with things. The family had denied her their secrets and she hers. She knew well the concept of them protecting her by holding back, but to give titbits of some grim history, snippets dangled in front of her, was just patronising.

Erica took the gun in both hands, holding it at arms length to take in its weight. A feeling like hysteria pulsed through her, from her groin to her face, and despite the cold, a solitary bead of sweat trickled down her back.

Monique couldn't have been the one to shut the kitchen door or make the place cold somehow; there would be perfume in the air if her presence had been recent. And Harry always left the kitchen door open to let the hall light shine through to the back of the house, so he wasn't the culprit either.

A excess of monthly hormones, a feeling that the last decade had been highly dissatisfactory — almost pointless — coupled with a devastating end to her evening at Janice's provided Erica with a sensation of joyous lunacy. Holding the gun was empowering. It was like stepping onto a film set, inhabiting another character; fooling around with it was personal retribution for what felt like an unremarkable journey to the age of twenty-six; it could even be another string to her bow of restitution.

Erica prised open the barrel, its mechanism sliding silently to reveal two dark passages. She loaded a couple of pellets and clicked it shut. There was no one in the house, this was just a bit of fun, the kind that made you sweat from pores previously unsoiled. It was self-defence against the self.

The front door creaked on its hinges in an icy draught, still open and drawing freezing air into the hall. Erica strode out of the dining room at once feeling ridiculous and in the same moment, reeling from the familiar sound of the back door hitting the dresser as it was opened.

She stared down the hall, eyelids peeled back, straining to hear more. Someone else was there, exiting, guilty of trespass. She was conscious of her toes pushing against the inside of her shoes, her bowels shifting nervously, and the brush of each fibre of her clothes against her skin. Erica made her way out and down the front steps, marching across the gravel to the side of the house.

She raised the gun to her shoulder and aimed roughly into the trees, mid height. The garden was in darkness and with her eyes not yet adjusted, inky and foreboding.

With a breath that seemed to freeze her chest, she fired twice, the shots causing her to wince with the force to her shoulder.

There was a sound like ice cracking deep inside a glacier, slow and crisp at first, then rising to a crescendo like a cascade of shattered icicles. A gaudy show of lurid green fireworks flew up from somewhere near the centre of the village and for a second, cast a dim illumination over the garden.

Erica saw Duncan in the last sputters of light, crouching in the greenhouse hands over his ears and eyes, blood and glass on his head and shoulders, his eyes screwed shut.

Connor's euphoria at having completed the marathon in three hours and thirteen minutes was quickly extinguished on his return to the UK. No sooner had his plane landed at Heathrow and his phone connected to a British network, than he received a series of messages from Erica explaining in curious terms that she needed to see him urgently, that there had been an accident.

Over the following days her neediness for his attention and the resulting explanation of events turned an innocent, carefully trodden and half-formed relationship into a meandering quagmire.

He had listened politely to how his girlfriend-cum-friend-cum-curiosity had fired a shotgun at her ex boyfriend, Duncan, who was hiding in her greenhouse one evening and whom she had mistaken for a more menacing intruder; how Duncan had got off lightly (because he shouldn't have been there in the first place and you could argue that he had got what was coming to him) with only fourteen stitches to his head and hands as a result of the greenhouse collapsing on him; how they had not involved the police; how Duncan's mother had flown down from Scotland and turned up screaming like a banshee at Harry on their front doorstep and how Monique had averted an impending act of violence against him by conversing (more than adequately and rather surprisingly) in Polish to diffuse the situation; and finally how her family and best friend Carmi, were now all treating her like she was some fragile object, slightly deranged, in need of some time off, but still not daring to approach the subject of the reason behind her momentary departure from her senses which was so obviously brought on by having discovered (or having *thought* she had discovered) the reason behind the family rift that had been so in evidence since her mother died suddenly ten years ago.

Connor had fed Erica Kleenex and gin to ease her through the detail. When she had finally remembered to ask him about the marathon, he had merely shrugged and said, "Yeah it was OK."

Over the following weeks, he was introduced to Harry, Erica's eldest sister Janice, Erica's brother-in-law and their kids. He was wheeled out as the bedrock for a normal, morally sound life: the new boyfriend is a police officer, how could anyone's judgement be possibly skewed on a permanent basis while dating someone with such a conventional career choice? Connor, during his first visit to the Old Rectory had held an embarrassing conversation with Harry about firearms and licences and was reassured that the gun had been 'donated' to a specialist auctioneer and the conversation was brought swiftly to a close.

When he had questioned Erica as to the reason for Duncan's presence in the house that night in the first place, she had been dismissive, saying that Duncan had meant no harm, to which Connor had responded in alarm.

"Aren't you worried that this idiot's going to try and break in again? That he might try and hurt you?"

"No, no. Duncan's soft. He won't be back, trust me. I work with him and I know him and we've spoken. It's OK."

Had Connor known Erica a little better he might have pursued this line further, questioning her reassurances, but in detecting that there was more to her dismissal of the subject than met the eye, decided to let it drop.

He made brief searches at work for criminal records on the family and on Duncan and had satisfied himself that the ex was probably just a harmless half-wit and that Erica's eccentric act was a one-off.

Everything had changed though. He had gone from genial acquaintance to full-blown boyfriend in a matter of days. Connor couldn't help feeling that he was being used to a certain degree as a prop to realign Erica with her family, a notion that he didn't wholly object to, not least because she was now sharing his bed. She was well meaning though, slightly less fragile than previously thought and possibly a little misunderstood. The act of firing the gun was a leap from the shy, traceless world of Erica Ford into the spotlight for a private audience – her family – and back again. Plus, she was evidently embarrassed by the whole thing and deeply sorry for having caused harm to Duncan. He was curious as to her eccentricity although he kept his barriers raised, commenting to his sister in Ireland that his consideration of Erica had elevated from 'moderately enigmatic' to 'a few fish short of a hatstand'.

Connor's sister had ummed and ahhed down the phone, adding darkly to "just be careful of that one".

Carmi on the other hand, whilst reacting to Erica in a light-hearted *you never did!* way, was poleaxed. She surprised Duncan by turning up at his flat the following weekend. Her eyes peering out from a clashing hat and scarf ensemble, Duncan had hesitated when he opened the door, not recognising her for a moment.

"Oh, hello."

"Hi. I heard about the accident and uh, well, can I come in?" She had walked purposefully past Duncan and into the kitchen. The place was spotless save for a few dirty mugs in the sink.

"Wow you really know how to keep a place ship shape." She said, unravelling her scarf and nodding to a faded framed poster on the wall. "I like the Klimt. Not seen that one before."

Duncan had hovered in the doorway dabbing at a lint patch over his eye.

"Did Erica send you?"

"No no. She doesn't know I'm here." Carmi got comfortable against the worktop and unravelled her scarf. "I'll cut to the chase. I'm worried about her. Worried about you too."

Duncan had frowned and instantly regretted it, wincing and holding his crown for a second or two.

"These bloody stitches, it's like having needles in your head."

"God. That's um. Yeah."

Carmi's relationship with Duncan had been forced over the years and she struggled to find empathy for him. They had liked each other on simple terms, acknowledging a shared basic ideology for life but had been at a loss with humour and warmth. She had thought Duncan dry and bumbling, wrapped up in his own work and emotionally restricted. Duncan had considered Carmi to be interfering and shallow, despite her academic success.

"What are you going to say when you go back to work?" She had ventured.

"I'll tell them I had plastic surgery or something. See if they pretend to notice a difference."

Carmi had smiled weakly considering the pattern that would be left behind on Duncan's balding head should he scar. "Seriously, are you going to tell people about it?"

"About what exactly? About the fact that I was loitering in Erica's greenhouse and she fired a gun at me? I don't think so."

"Sorry, God, sorry. I didn't mean that to sound... well, I didn't mean to pry." Carmi walked over to Duncan, her high boots clipping the tiles, and placed her hand awkwardly on his arm.

"You didn't mean to pry? Carmi, why are you here?" Duncan had asked sounding worn out with the visit already.

"Well…"

"Look I don't know what I'm going to say, probably that I got into a fight or had an accident or something. I've been signed off for a fortnight and my boss is being cool about it. No heavy questions, that kind of thing. So I'm going to worry about that next week. If I get signed off for longer – which I doubt I will – I might go up to Scotland for a bit. Mum's already been down but she had to get back to work."

"Yes, I heard." Carmi had taken up her former position at the opposite side of the room, refracted winter sunlight warming her skin.

"So you're worried about Erica." Duncan said flatly. "I don't think you're here 'cos you're worried about me."

Carmi exhaled loudly and shoved her hands into her coat pockets.

"I'm not one for keeping secrets from my best friend Duncan, but I'd be grateful if we kept this conversation between ourselves." Carmi hesitated and looked to Duncan for agreement.

He nodded.

"Good. Thank you." She paused. "Duncan, what were you doing at Erica's house that night? Erica's playing it down big time, but she must have been bloody scared to have used a gun."

"Bloody mental if you ask me." Duncan muttered.

"Erica's not *mental*. You're just lucky she didn't call the police."

"Lucky? I've got a dozen stitches in my head! The only fortunate thing about any of it was when the paramedics believed the story that the green house had collapsed due to an exceptionally loud firework."

"I mean Duncan, that you could have been arrested for burglary and what with all the break-ins lately, well, it's a bit of a stupid position to put yourself in, don't you think?"

"Who are you? My mother?"

"God Duncan, I didn't come here to row with you."

Duncan remained quiet for a moment, his eyes flitting around the room.

"Look, we both care about her, which is why I'm here and presumably why you broke into her house last weekend." Carmi looked at him levelly until he caught her eye. "Although I can only assume you've taken the meaning of 'caring' to the next level."

"Jesus Carmi, I'm not a friggin stalker. I was worried about her and about Harry. I think he's been ill. And I think she's been seeing some other guy and it totally did my head in and I realised that we'd made a big mistake when we split up so I just went round there on an impulse to sort things out. To get to the bottom of things you know? I also leant her a laptop ages ago and I wanted it back, I wanted to give it to my mum."

This last part of the account sounded contrived and Carmi had looked at Duncan squarely, narrowing her eyes.

"Why did you break in though?"

"I didn't. The door was open so I went in."

"But you must have known no one was in – it's pretty easy to tell if there are no cars in the drive."

"Yes but the lights were on so I put my bike round the side and went up to the door. I walked in, noticed no one was about and then I heard a car on the drive and I shat it."

Carmi had considered Duncan's posture for second: miserable, almost grovelling.

"Go on."

"I hid in the kitchen for a bit and then left through the back door. And then I heard footsteps round the side and then, well. The rest is history."

"Indeed." Carmi had said.

"I felt terrible Carmi, I really did. But then when she fired the gun at me – *Jesus.*"

"She didn't fire the gun *at* you, she didn't know you were there."

"It was Guy Fawkes, there were fireworks all over the shop. It certainly wasn't pitch dark."

"Duncan, Erica did not *see* you in the greenhouse. Let's get that straight. She thought you were the burglar. She *thought*..." Carmi sighed. "That taking matters into her own hands was the right thing to do."

"OK OK. But still. It was a bit rash."

Carmi rubbed her forehead vigorously, searchingly. "Yes... but you know when people have suffered themselves somehow... previously. Well you can sort of see how you might want to rebel against your own fear. Prove something to yourself."

Duncan looked blank.

"OK. It was a bit out of character."

"You're not wrong."

They both stood in silence, a large plastic wall clock marking the time in steady clicks.

"So that's it then? That's all there is to it?" Carmi had asked.

"Yup."

Carmi left shortly after, ninety percent satisfied that the whole thing was a dreadful accident and that Duncan was even more of a hapless idiot that she had previously thought. He had acted stupidly and without malice and that was the most important thing to establish. The remaining ten percent of her that was still dissatisfied with the explanation, she put to one side, logic and probability denying her the difficulty of dwelling on it for too long.

SEVENTEEN

Just as the incident with Duncan was beginning to feel a little less raw, a surprising thing happened.

Erica was at her desk, humming to herself and absorbed in her work, when the phone rang. It was Connor calling from the office.

"Hello you." He said boldly. "I have some information that you might be interested in."

Erica sat up straight, smiling. "Oh really?"

"I just ran another search on those villages and postcodes you gave me ages ago and it seems like there's been a change. Maybe there's something in this electricity pylon stuff after all."

"Ah." Said Erica and swivelled to face the window, her smile diminishing. The clouds looked heavy enough to snow and all the offices were lit despite being midday. "What exactly have you found?" She asked gently.

"A bit of a change since last month. That's for sure. More so than any average fluctuation could account for."

"I see. I see." Erica said slowly. "I can't really talk too much now." She added staring out of the window, eyes flicking to the smears on the outside of the glass.

"Do you want me to print some of this stuff for you? Assuming you still want it."

"Oh yes please. Do."

"It's quite a drop. I mean not in actual numbers, because these aren't huge populations of people to start with, but percentage-wise, or however you'd describe it statistically, it's significant. A lot less violence. I mean a *lot* less."

"Right." Erica ran her hand through her hair. Her activities at the brewery had taken a back seat while things were smoothed over at home and with Duncan.

"Right." She repeated. "I'll catch up with you about it later."

"You would have thought that being close to electrical fluctuations might inflame people or agitate them, not calm them down." Connor continued, his voice trailing in thought. "You are thinking of seasonal fluctuations aren't you?" He added hopefully.

"Yes that's right." Erica confirmed quickly. "With the nights drawing in, there's more power being consumed."

She had elaborated on the reasons for her research when Connor had recently pressed her. This had involved explaining that not only did she want to explore the connection between the proximity of people to power lines and their tendencies for violence, but how this could change with the alterations in the levels of energy being transported. The project was 'research on the side' – she couldn't possibly justify her time spent at the office working on this sort of thing as it was outside of her remit by a whole job description. However, if she could get something published, it might open up new opportunities for her. Connor had applauded Erica's apparent approach to self development but queried that there might be an easier way of moving careers i.e. by simply applying for a different job or studying a course. She was working in the Science faculty after all.

"I think you're on to something though." He continued. "So why don't we see this sort of thing during thunderstorms? You'd think everyone would be chilled out when it's stormy, but that's never the case. It's like full moons – people really do go crazy. Accident and Emergency is packed and so are our cells."

"That sort of change is more to do with atmospheric pressure and the increase in static electricity people experience during storms. It's a different kind of electrical force anyway." Said Erica, staging the confidence in her voice.

"And why not this change every winter? I know people go nuts at Christmas but that's social factors and alcohol, isn't it?"

Erica tore off a ragged nail with her teeth and spat it quietly to the floor.

"I agree. But with all the new housing developments and a rise in the population, the electrical infrastructure's being pushed. I've got my eye on a journal I'd like to submit to. Nothing huge, but it'd be a foot in. Might even get a proper research project out of it if there's any cash sloshing around at the end of the year." She swung round to face her computer again. "I've really got to go Connor. I've got stuff to finish before lunch. But thanks for calling."

Erica knew that to make the assumption that anyone with an artistic bent such as Connor, was less likely to see the flaws in scientifically-based arguments or conjecture, was foolish. It was possible for a person to pursue a decent understanding of science *and* the arts; the two weren't mutually exclusive in everyone even though they were in her, and most evidently, in Duncan.

She spoke with as much alacrity as she could muster on the subject when pressed by Connor but preferred to stay off it altogether, wary of the limits of her own knowledge and the plausibility of it all. He was too inquisitive to let new theories pass unquestioned and Erica's only release from tight corners was to change the subject. There had been enough explaining to do lately.

"OK, well I'll take this stuff home with me tonight." Said Connor to break the brief silence. "You coming over later?"

"Um. Not sure. I think I'm visiting dad at the brewery." Erica said clicking through a spreadsheet on her computer distractedly. "I'll call you when I'm finished here."

The afternoon passed slowly, Erica dithering over her work and ignoring the opportunity of coffee with Carmi at three.

She revisited the websites from which she had bought the last batch of drugs and continued to gnaw at her nails as Connor's news bored into her brain. It had felt at times like child's play, like making mud pies in the garden, but with no real expectation that the resultant mash would resemble the one in her imagination. Or rather, Erica had not prepared herself for the possibility that her own juvenile concoction of very adult ingredients might actually achieve the intended result. She thought she ought to feel euphoric at this stage, but instead was caught up with worrying about what to do next.

Duncan had been back at work for a week and had kept the reason for his injuries a secret as he had promised Erica he would. They agreed that it would benefit neither of them to reveal the truth of Guy Fawkes night to anyone other than family and a few friends, namely Carmi and Duncan's flatmate, Andy. He had healed quickly, his scars pink and taught, pin prinks of the dissolved stitches peppering his pale head in neat rows. The explanation he gave to colleagues was brief and jocular: he had been at a bonfire party with friends in London when an out of control firework had brought down the greenhouse he was sheltered in. It really wasn't all that sore at first – the most painful part had been the stitches.

Duncan continued to explain that he had tacked on some annual leave to his recovery time because the whole experience had been a bit of a shock to him and he'd decided to spend some time in Glasgow with his mother.

He was the talk of the office for the first day he was back, his story mercifully eclipsed that same morning by the news that a former reality TV contestant had been offered a late place on an earth sciences course and could be found making coffee in the Science Faculty common room.

Anita Singh however, had pursued Erica for details shortly after Duncan's return to work. Erica had cut her short, reminding her curtly that Duncan wasn't her boyfriend any more. Her boss had frowned, cocking her head disbelievingly, an act which vexed Erica so much that she had relayed it on to Carmi as soon as she could.

The end of the month felt like a welcomed turning point towards Christmas – the weirdness of November could be put to bed.

By five o'clock it was completely dark outside and felt for all the world like bedtime. Erica drove quickly to the brewery and got there early enough to talk briefly to staff, glad of the friendly and benign banter offered by familiar faces. Boxes of Christmas decorations lay unpacked in the small the reception area and Erica knelt down to rifle through them as she waited for Harry. The ritual at the brewery was to spend the first working day of December decorating a tree and hanging lights about the place, something that he had made the children wait torturously for at home; Erica's parents had always left decorations untouched until Christmas Eve which was at odds with the brewery tradition.

Erica pulled out a handful of ball-balls and a shabby white fairy wrapped in cotton wool, as big and round as a football. Decorations had moved between the brewery and the Old Rectory over the years and the fairy was one such relic. Erica smoothed its satin dress, roughly cut and unhemmed, and struggled to recall how she had helped Janice and her mother make it all those years ago. She closed her eyes to call up her mother's face in her mind, but instead was drawn to an image of the hefty Singer sewing machine that had produced the fairy's dress – and all hers – in the Eighties.

Her clothes had been created from paper patterns, bulging and stuffed into short white envelopes, pencil drawings of slender women posing on the front. Dorothy had chosen the designs and the girls had selected the fabrics. Ellen had been the only one to resist. As a full eight years older than Erica, she had been embarrassed to be wearing her mother's creations from the age of ten. Janice had been more giving about her outfits partly because she was an overtly late developer when it came to teenage fashion and partly so as not to offend when the clothes did bother her.

Erica opened her eyes, aware of footsteps on the stairwell, put the ball-balls back into the box and stuffed the tatty fairy into her bag.

Harry sauntered in, his feet dragging on the floorboards.

"Hi love." He said. "Thought that was your car outside."

"Hiya." Erica hugged her father. "God you look tired dad." She said looking into his eyes. His hair was overdue a trim and was splayed in frizzy twists from his head.

"You know how it is at this time of the year." Said Harry, nodding towards the boxes on the floor.

"Well, that's kind of why I'm here." Said Erica, her face eager. "Wondered if you needed a hand with anything."

Harry stroked Erica's arm lightly and shuffled towards his office.

"I'm all done here for the day love. I was going to take some stuff home with me though, paperwork mainly."

"I can help you with that." Said Erica lightly. "I've got nothing on."

"Not seeing that new chap of yours?" Harry smiled.

"Connor? No. Not tonight." She hovered by Harry's office door and watched him slowly shifting about the room, a sadness breaking out over her to see the weariness in his movements. Was it work that had made him so these last few weeks, or was it the stress she had caused him? She bit her lip, disappointed in herself for not having considered the possibility that the shotgun incident may have taken more of a toll on Harry than just a few anxious nights. He could be carrying the weight of it all silently; he could even have some knowledge of the row at Janice's and the awful things that had been said there. She hadn't said anything about it, too consumed by the whole clean-up operation to tackle Janice's comments about her father.

Harry dragged a mess of papers strewn on his desk into an untidy pile and kept his head down.

"I've been so busy here lately love, I've hardly had a chance to think about anything else. I'm sorry. I hope you haven't been thinking I've neglected you."

Erica shook her head, worry falling away from her in slabs.

"Good." He smiled. "I don't think there's much in the fridge. Shall we stop by the chippie on the way back?"

"Yeah. Let's do that." Erica beamed and collected up the papers. "I'll sort these schedules out for you when we get home – OK?"

EIGHTEEN

Harry sat at the end of the dining table, cupping his sixth glass of red wine in his long, bony hands. He was smiling because he had had two days away from the brewery for the first time in as many months and because Monique had prepared an exquisite meal. Monique was kneeling by the fire, inexpertly shifting a log into the flames from the edge of the grate and laughing at her own clumsiness. It was an unusual scene — a first since Dorothy had gone — that any member of the Ford family had lit a fire, let alone dine, in the old room. Candles dribbled in brass candelabras on the mantelpiece, two empty wine bottles were adrift in the middle of the long mahogany table and a steady pulse of syncopated tango rhythms emanated from an aging stereo.

Contrary to Erica's concerns, Harry hadn't been overly distressed by the incident on Guy Fawkes night. The damage to Duncan's head was of immediate concern and the visit paid by his mother was plain annoying, but he had dealt with it all without too much question: Duncan was a harmless soul, known and trusted; Monique had truly had a blond moment when she'd left the front door open; and Erica was, it was now evident, prone to over-reaction. Harry's sister had hollered at him over the phone that he was spending too much time at work and not enough with his family adding that it was not normal for young people to resort to firearms in times of need, unless, she had said, they were part of some despicable gang. Was she getting through to him?

Harry had taken this on board for the duration of the call, promising time out with Erica after Christmas and then at once relieved of the duty of any requisite counselling by the appearance of the new boyfriend. He was definitely handy to have on the scene and Harry hoped would help to detract Erica's attention from life at home while he indulged in spending what little spare time he had with Monique.

He had edged around Monique as delicately as he could, curious about her at first, flattered by her attention but keeping a distance that he felt appropriate for a landlord. She took on favours for him and vice versa; it was an easy co-existence in the Old Rectory and one that Harry dared not read anything deeper into.

It was Monique's suggestion that they use the dining room that evening and Harry welcomed the invigorating spirit of entertainment that she bestowed upon them when they found themselves with time to kill. It was a welcomed departure from an evening in the pub.

"You know what I like about you Harry?" Asked Monique moving back to her seat.

"What?"

"You're not always correcting my bloody English."

They both giggled a little, a natural continuation of an upbeat discourse that they had enjoyed over dinner.

"Some of the people I work with you know, it's like they're hardly listening to what I am *actually* saying and concentrating instead on *how* I am saying it. I'm a bloody French teacher for God's sake – I know a thing or two about grammar. The fact that I'm able to teach history as well they should just be damn grateful for."

"Indeed, indeed." Agreed Harry, affecting a more well-to-do tone than was natural for him, one that often came into play when drinking wine.

"Like this woman the other day, the PE teacher of all things. She says to me, she says 'Moni*ca*' – always Monica, like she can't stop anglicising everything – she says 'Moni*ca*, I think you'll find the place you're referring to is pronounced *Slough*, as in *cow*, not *sluff*.' Good lord! I've lived here for twenty years, of course I know how it's pronounced. Does she think I'm stupid? I'm just bringing in my own take on the pronunciation of English towns, and one that I consider to be conversationally amusing. It's like, because English isn't my first language, I'm not capable of humour with deliberate mispronunciation!"

"Oh dear." Said Harry frowning.

"And this is after I've explained about something of particular relevance to her function as the PE teacher. She wasn't actually listening to the content of my narrative, just the delivery – argh!" Monique took a long sip of wine and then leant into the table, her cheeks twitching with a smile. "So you know what I said?"

Harry shook his head.

"I said 'Thank you Carolin*a* —'"

The front door opened and Erica walked in, hunched and weary, dragging her bag at arms length along the floor.

"Oh Erica, hi!" Monique stood up. "I've saved you some food. Sit down, sit down."

Erica, briefly propped against the door frame of the dining room was ushered to a place set for her, complete with artistically folded napkin. Monique marched off to the kitchen, her wedge-heeled slippers slapping at her heels with a dainty snip-snip.

"Wow." Said Erica, sitting down heavily, her coat hanging off one shoulder. "This looks grand."

Harry considered for a second the discomfort he felt when faced with justifying any time spent with Monique. Adequately lubricated, he tried to let the feeling slide and reached out to clasp Erica's hand.

"Monique's made a lovely meal. You'll like it." He urged, squeezing her fingers.

"Cool." She said assertively and slid her coat off on to the back of the chair. "Can't remember the last time we lit a fire in here."

"I know, I know. Isn't it great?" It doesn't draw so well that one, but the smell of wood smoke in the house is rather nice I think." He looked at the fireplace as if to examine it and then back into Erica's face, searching for approval. She said nothing but smiled politely.

"How was the brewery?" He asked.

"Oh fine. I finished the paperwork ages ago but I ended up helping Saul with the stock take." Erica yawned. *"And then Connor came to meet me on his break so the three of us had a quick pint in the King's Arse."*

Harry grinned and leant back into his seat. "Oh good."

"That Saul's a really nice bloke isn't he?" Continued Erica. "Shy at first I thought, but seems like he's got his heart in the right place."

"I know, I know. He's a gem. Just given him a pay rise actually. I don't want him leaving as soon as the apprenticeship's over." Harry paused, fiddling with the stem of his glass and then added as an afterthought. "I'll pay you love. For today. I don't expect this to be charity work. The brewery makes enough to do that. Hundred quid OK? Cash."

"Whatever." Erica shrugged. "God your cheeks are red dad."

"Oh?" Harry patted his face and smiled. "Too much of the good stuff. Let me pour you some. Looks like we need another bottle." Harry poured the dregs into Erica's glass and caught a smile rising further on one side of her face. "What?"

"You're pissed."

"Me?" Harry's smile broadened, exacerbating the broken veins in his cheeks.

"Oh dear. One night off and look at the state of you." Erica raised her glass in salute. "Nice one." She said.

Monique marched back in, placing a dish of steaming lasagne in front of Erica and thumped a fresh bottle of wine on the table. "I'll get the rest." She bustled out again and returned with a small salad and half a loaf of ciabatta. "There's garlic butter in the bread. And mind – it's hot." She said cheerily. "You better eat some now so you don't notice how much me and your dad already stink."

"I will. This looks gorgeous. Thanks."

Harry relaxed, a feeling of contentment settling through his bones. Domestic harmony had been a rare beast in the Old Rectory after Guy Fawkes night and the convivial atmosphere nourished him.

"I was just rattling on to your dad – or was I prattling? Sprattling? Rattling." Said Monique directing her enthusiasm at Erica.

"Sprattling's good." Offered Harry. "I like that."

"About school, you know. How people form prejudices about you, or make assumptions based on your looks or where you're from."

"Same the world over I would have thought." Said Erica blowing onto a forkful of molten cheese and pasta.

"Yes, but you would think that the staff room of a school would be a more relaxing place to be because of the people you expect to find there: slightly left of centre, the hard done bys, the over-worked, you know? It should be somewhere you can have an intelligent conversation without scrutiny or feeling like you're having to set an example."

"They're a shallow bunch then." Erica confirmed.

"God yes. It's part of the reason I left Birmingham. Well, one of the reasons, a small one." Monique tailed off for a second. "But I did think I might find more enlightenment in a smaller, more *posh* part of the UK." She picked up again, looking into Harry's face brightly. "Not so." She said.

Monique plunged a cork screw into a fresh bottle of burgundy and twisted it down forcefully through the plastic cork. Her thick blond hair fell over her face and she pulled at the neck, heaving until her head flipped back with the effort of releasing the cork, revealing her flushed face.

"You'd think I'd have a better technique by now. I'm not really very French. I didn't even like red wine until I was in my thirties."

"Unlike me and beer." Said Harry, happy to interject with a merry nugget. "I was practically weaned on the stuff."

"Yes and a good job it doesn't make you fat. For some reason it doesn't touch the sides with you dad." Erica chipped in.

"So where was I?" Monique went on, decanting the wine. "So I'm trying to get a discussion going in the staff room about this, um, multiplicity principle. That there's more than one way of looking at things, that understanding the truth of something requires getting past the perspective through which it's portrayed. In the teaching context that is. And how I'd been trying to get this through in my history class that morning, you know, to open up the subject a bit more, because of a lot of it can be quite dull. Especially the World Wars. God, don't talk to me about that. The set books have hardly changed since I was at school. Very dry." She paused to take a long sip of her fresh glass revealing bluish lips. "And do you know what this guy says to me – Assistant Head and all? He says 'That'll never get them through their GCSEs dear.' *Dear!*" Monique tapped her index finger on the table while imitating her colleague. "'Got to stick to the programme.' Forget about the real value of education, giving kids something to think about beyond the syllabus."

"Did you tell him what for?" Asked Harry his eyes drooping, following the basic emphasis of Monique's speech but having gone adrift towards the end.

"God yes. I un*leashed* myself upon him."

Erica and Harry laughed loudly, Erica finding it impossible to keep her mouth closed.

"He saw the full wrath of a woman who knows a bit more about the philosophies of educating children than a dead-from-the-neck-up has-been, counting the days to his retirement."

"Was he a prat?" Ask Harry.

"Yes! A prat." Monique pushed the hair off her face, the flush from her cheeks barely subsided. "He is prat*tish*. A sprattling prat of a man."

"A sprat." Offered Erica.

Monique roared.

"Yes, a sprat! Grey, wriggling and slimy." She held up her hand and moved her little finger up and down as if to suggest the movement of a small fish. The gesture was also the universal symbol for indicating a small penis, which the three recognised instantly.

"Oh." Said Harry childishly, unsure of whether to acknowledge the mistake.

Erica looked down at her plate still smiling and fiddled with her food. Monique shot Harry an inquisitive look across the table, raising an eyebrow as a question mark and biting her lip. He stared back at her, eyes glazed, smiling blandly, hiding behind his inebriation.

A buzzer went off in the kitchen, chirping agitatedly and Monique went after it muttering about dessert. Harry tore a chunk of bread from Erica's plate and stuffed it greedily into his mouth, filling his cheeks like an overfed hamster, puffing and laughing through his nose.

NINETEEN

A detached stone cottage on the edge of the Cotswolds. A cloudless midwinter day. Frost lingering in sunless patches. Plastic boxes of recycling stuffed with torn up wrapping paper and cardboard tucked by the wall of the long front garden. The kitchen, spotless, dishes wiped and piled, ready to be put away, bins emptied, blinds drawn, floors swept. Erica stared out of the window to the half a dozen or so other houses in the hamlet, human occupancy marked by the presence of four-wheel drives parked outside. A power cut on Christmas Eve had knocked everyone's Christmas lights timers out of synch which made it even more evident which residents were in and those that were away for the holidays.

Inhabitants waved occasionally in this semi-neighbourhood, but with the absence of a shop or a pub, the place had all the social charm you would expect from a desolate cluster of buildings on a narrow B-road, despite their vernacular appeal. It was a road that led only to other amenity-free villages, connecting them in their nestled clusters amid the undulating eggshell topography of the limestone hills.

No wonder Cleo went spare out here. This was no place for a young woman to spend her twentieth year. Still, people might think the same thing of a twenty-six-year-old living at home with their dad.

She thought about what she might say to Cleo: *This is your family home and it will always be. If Janice and your dad move, no matter. It will remain always in your heart. But leave now, take the route that Ellen took, live a little and be free. And for God's sake, quit the country drinking set and get a taste of a city before it's too late.*

Erica was disturbed by a thud from above and the clatter of the twins bringing armfuls of toys down the stairs. She had woken early and tidied the place, deciding at the precise moment of waking that she would depart as soon as

Janice was up. Killing time was easy but there was nothing left to clean or pack. She looked over to her small case and a silver gift bag stuffed with her Christmas presents that stood by the front door. She fiddled with her key ring around her thumb, a habit she was not conscious of having. It was eleven o'clock in the morning on the day after Boxing Day and Janice and Keith were still in bed. The boys had spent the morning in their room laying train tracks, and Cleo had hit the sales with her Christmas money.

She plucked the retro digital radio from the kitchen windowsill and padded into the lounge to see the boys.

"Auntie Erica, my transformer's gonna land on the back of the sofa, like this, and then it's going to…" Benedict paused, wrenching the plastic figure apart. "… do this."

Erica squatted with them on the floor, searching for something lively on the radio.

"Do they dance Ben?" She asked. "Like in the advert?"

She picked up an abandoned transformer and began to twist it into shape.

"That's mine!" Said Casper boisterously, snatching it off her.

"Oh!" Said Erica brightly. *Jesus. Get me away from these spoilt brats.*

She turned the radio up and fiddled with her mobile, re-reading a series of texts from friends and family all wishing her a Happy Christmas, embellished with rows of kisses and exclamation marks. She lingered on one from Duncan that said he was drunk and that he missed her.

"I don't like that music." Said Casper, reaching out for the radio.

Erica put her hand out to stop him and without looking up, said, "Tough."

They had had enough of each other.

Christmas was, as it usually was, a broken up affair. A series of invitations had been issued and passed like Chinese whispers among the family and extended family. Harry had, of course, invited everyone to the Old Rectory for Christmas day, and everyone had declined in a roundabout sort of way. If the matrix of siblings and aunts wasn't yet fixed, it was easier to decline than to risk finding yourself part of a forced combination of people who shared varying degrees of love and tolerance for each other. Janice had been the first to decline but had promised to bring the whole family over to Brenly some time during Christmas week. She in turn, had put Erica in a difficult position by inviting her over. Harry had been asked to spend a few days in Wales with his sister who was becoming prematurely frail but had had to put off his decision while he waited to find out what Erica was doing, and then secretly, Monique. Ellen, alternating her movements from year to year, was due to spend a testing couple of days in the company of Francoise's family which included fielding the politically incorrect outbursts of the resident grandmother. (The invitation was extended to Erica by Ellen's request, who had suggested that she might enjoy a different scene and in doing so help her to form a more stable alliance for the duration.) Erica had found herself as usual, torn between allegiances to her sisters and to Harry, escaping everyone the previous year by spending Christmas morning in Duncan's flat playing computer games, drinking champagne and eating chocolate before breakfast. Harry's invitation to Connor to spend Christmas day at the Old Rectory was declined without hesitation, Erica's feelings then further damaged by there being absolutely no mention of the possibility of her accompanying him to Northern Ireland. She tried not to bother herself with these facts; it was early days after all. As it was, Monique chose last minute to visit siblings in France, Erica persuaded Harry to go to his sister's and having done so, agreed to spend the highlight of the festive period in the outback with Janice.

    An hour passed and Janice emerged zipping a pair of loose-fitting jeans as she walked down the stairs.

    "Hiya." Erica marched swiftly into the kitchen. "I'll put the kettle on."

"Morning. I fell back to sleep." Said Janice leaning down to rub the boys' heads who were by then, engrossed in the television. "Must have needed it."

"I'm gonna head Janice. I'm meeting Carmi for coffee in town and then maybe for a bit of shopping." Erica pulled a large, chipped teapot out of the cupboard and threw a couple of tea bags into it. "Which is where Cleo is, incidentally."

"Huh?"

"Shopping."

"Crikey. She didn't waste any time." Janice spoke through a yawn and sat down heavily at the kitchen table ignoring the marathon of cleaning that had taken place. She picked at her nails and then at a spot on the table. Erica watched, propped against a cupboard, arms folded, detecting that her sister was either still only semi conscious or dwelling on something altogether unrelated to Cleo's outing. Rather than pursue small talk, she chose to depart.

"Thanks for a lovely few days." She hugged her, inhaling the comforting residue of yesterday's perfume.

"You're not staying for a cuppa?"

"No, gotta go." Erica was hungry for lunch and could have assembled something tasty from Christmas leftovers. Instead she walked into the lounge and kissed the boys on the backs of their heads, Benedict surprising her by turning round and delivering a tight squeeze around her waist. She laughed, filling up with love for him all over again, like the day she had first held him as a baby, and kissed him a second time. Detecting that Casper still had the hump, she left him alone.

Erica hauled on her heavy coat and opened the front door.

"See you guys soon." She called to the boys.

"What do you say?" Called Janice in her matronly way from the kitchen.

"Bye Auntie Erica." The boys chimed spinning round from their floor spot momentarily to deliver gappy smiles. Erica waved back from the hall and then turned to Janice.

"See you at dad's then."

"Huh?" Janice rubbed her eyes.

"You said you'd bring everyone over this week."

Janice looked back at her sister blankly.

"Let me know which day you're planning as I need to get the shopping in."

"Yeah." Janice yawned again looking down at the hall floor, somewhere around Erica's feet.

"Promise?"

"Promise."

Janice called out as an afterthought as Erica was closing the door.

"Bye honey. Thanks for everything."

During the course of the day, a number of the Ford family members made a number of exceptional discoveries. The first was Harry's. He had synchronised his return from his sister's with Monique's from France, the plan being that they could enjoy good food, long walks and the company of Harry's daughters and grandchildren while the festive mood was still upon them. At midday, Harry bounded through the front door laden with bags, groceries and a dozen bottles of beer that he'd picked up on his way back past the brewery. The house was quiet and cool, curtains half drawn to reveal lights on the Christmas tree from the front window, draining boards and sinks were dry and bare. He dumped his luggage in the hall and walked into the kitchen to engage the central heating system and to put the kettle on, rubbing his hands briskly with the satisfaction of being home and the anticipation of good company. The boiler burst into life purring with hot gas, pushing water around the house and bringing every room to life with the clicks of expanding pipe work. Harry paused again in the hall, hands on hips – take a pee or light a fire first? Deciding on the latter he walked into the lounge and hunkered down by the fireplace.

He pulled at the grate to inspect the ash, becoming aware of a sound like the floorboards shifting with the pressure of footsteps. The hairs on the back of Harry's head bristled and he had swivelled on his haunches to turn to face whatever was moving behind him. He was toppled by a blow to his arm that he had instinctively held up against his face and fell completely to his knees with a smack.

"I've come for what's mine." Said a man's voice, emanating from Harry's view, from the top of a pair of eighteen-hole Dr Marten boots.

There was another blow across his back and the unmistakable sensation of a foot shoving him down.

Pain seared through his eye sockets and to his cheeks and blood poured out through his nose. He had fallen in to the fireplace face-first.

This was the moment that he later tried to pick apart for Monique and then for Erica, the aching seconds that followed and the curious acceptance of what was happening to him. He'd been in enough trouble in his youth to know that he was easily riled. But as his attacker stepped back and Harry floundered from his knees to take comfort on the sagging leather footstool, there was no equivalent torment goading him to lash out. Instead, he took his breath and announced, panting and sniffing – "Take what you want."

Harry, unsure whether there would be another blow, kept his head down, eyes fixed on the man's boots. The intruder hesitated and Harry heard the sound of the antique carriage clock being swept from the mantelpiece into an already swollen rucksack.

"I didn't want to hurt you Harry. But this has gone on too long. It'll be over soon."

Within the event, that had so far lasted only a minute or so, Harry made his second discovery. He had recognised the pair of black leather boots that had so consumed his vision from the fireplace.

After only an hour with Carmi holed up in Starbucks, hugging fat mugs bristling with hot chocolate and melted marshmallows, Erica's phone rang. She angled the screen to read the caller's identity.

"I better get this – it's dad."

"Go for it." Carmi shuffled off the long red sofa and collected spent plates and muffin papers from the table.

"Hi dad."

"Hi Erica. It's me – Monique."

"Oh hi." Erica sucked at a sugary teaspoon. "I'm just in town with Carmi. I'll be back tonight. I've left Janice's so I was heading home later. Did you have a nice time?"

There was a short silence and then Monique spoke quietly.

"Yes, lovely. Um, Erica, could you pop back a bit earlier?"

Erica sat forward and frowned. "Yeah. What's up?"

More silence.

"Oh something's come up."

She strained to listen for background noise but caught only the hiss of the phone line.

"Your dad's here. He just got back himself." Monique added. "So, well... we need you to... well, I think you should come home now."

"What, *right* now?"

"Yes please. It's quite important."

Erica blanched taking in the possibility of Harry's disappointment, his shame, of having discovered her foolery at the brewery somehow, so gutted for his daughter's behaviour that he couldn't bring himself to call her directly. She saw herself standing before him in confession, and then to the police, to Janice, Connor, the whole lot of them.

Erica shook her head to banish the thought. She needed time to collect herself, prepare her speech, responses, lies, whatever it took to explain or convince them of her innocence.

Monique interrupted her meandering thoughts.

"Tell Carmi I'm ever so sorry."

"What is it Monique? You're freaking me out."

Carmi slid back along the sofa and faced her friend, frowning and mouthing *'Is he OK?'*

Erica shrugged feebly.

"I'll tell you when you get here. Don't worry though. We're all OK. No one's in trouble. No one's died."

These words had a small but significantly calming effect on Erica whose pulse had increased in pace and pressure.

"OK, well I'm parked in the Westgate, so it'll take fifteen minutes to get there and to get out, so I reckon I'll be back…" Erica tucked the tiny phone under her chin and wrenched her sleeve back to see her watch. "…around three."

"That's fine. See you then."

Erica drank from her mug in forced swallows.

"I gotta go. Monique's all weirded out about something and wants me home now."

"Oh. Why?"

"Dunno. She wouldn't say. Said she's there with dad but I couldn't hear him. They've both just got back."

Erica took a final gulp of chocolate and pulled on her coat awkwardly.

"So why did Monique have to ring you?"

Erica, not comprehending the question stopped moving and stared at her friend. "Oh *god*."

"What?"

Her face was paler than usual, her mouth open."

"*What?*" Asked Carmi again.

"Nothing, no…no." She muttered, getting to her feet. She slung her bag over her shoulder which promptly slid down her arm, and wrestled in her pockets for her car keys. "God I'm sorry Carmi. I gotta dash. It sounded urgent."

"I can tell. You're talking weird and you're white as a sheet." She pulled her friend in briefly and kissed her cheek. "Call me, OK?"

The roads were already refreezing when Erica left town and she drove at a speed that was disrespectful of their potential to send her spinning into a hedgerow. The journey to Brenly took in two hamlets and a narrow bank of hills – the last rumble of The Chilterns before the descent into the Oxford basin. Trees arranged in neat rectangles formed a distraction from barren tracts of farmland, their silhouettes overwhelmed by fat ivy fronds that strangled their trunks. The last to hold on to their drying foliage in the mild winter were oak and the head-turning copper beech. One such specimen stood alone in the centre of a steeply sloping field given over to endless crops of rapeseed. Mature, broad and over a hundred feet tall, it pleased Erica each time she saw it to note that throughout the year the tree was ploughed around – revered in circles of furrowed earth: first lines of green shoots, followed by livid yellow and back to green. It was a nod to aesthetics over maximum yield per hectare, a nudge to lift the spirits at each passing, but cast aside this particular journey, acknowledged only in her peripheral vision.

The stretch between the hamlets was always the worst for road kill: tight bends flanked by acres of farmland and broad coppices that housed most of central England's species, all of which felt bound to cross the road at some point in their lives. It was common to see fluffy flat streaks of carrion, the occasional ear or feather standing to attention from its levelled body, flapping in the breeze.

Taking the brow of the hill and turning into this exposed stretch at too great a speed to be in control, Erica saw the carcass of god-knows-what in the centre of the road. Three red kites were picking at it, wings half extended, dancing from end to end on its body. It was rare to see kites close up, the most usual sighting was from the ground up as they wove in tight circles to search for carrion from hundreds of feet up. The dipped angle of the sun caught the birds' bodies full on, revealing a blaze of chestnut red. With the rapidly closing gap between her and the feeding frenzy, the sight was both sumptuous and agitating. She pumped the brakes, wary of skidding, asserting instantly that she could not stop in time. With less than a second between them, the kites rose up on an invisible tide, riding with their two-metre wingspans over the bonnet of Erica's car, inches from the windscreen, sailing with the aerodynamics of the vehicle. Spectacular as it was to be so proximal to the great birds, Erica screamed and brought the car though zigzags to a halt. She panted, hands tight and clammy on the wheel to observe the kites in her mirror, back to their task of stripping the carcass from the road, apparently unscathed by their own brush with mortality.

The lights of the Old Rectory were ablaze on the ground floor, eager and indulgent at sunset.

"I'm home." Erica said as she walked in, invoking a forced joviality in the face of the unknown. She found Harry and Monique in the kitchen, Harry sitting upright in the largest of the pine chairs, Monique on the table, cupping a mug of tea, legs swaying in agitated thrusts. There was no music, no fires lit and the occupants' bags were still lined up in the hallway from their recent return to the house.

Monique slid off the table, and walking past Erica towards the kettle, noiselessly squeezed her on the shoulder. It took Erica a couple of seconds to notice the damage to Harry's face, the contents of their aging first aid box strewn on the table top and the manner in which Harry cradled his left arm, as if it were a wounded pet.

Erica was momentarily speechless. She bent towards him, examining the bruises to his face, not knowing how or whether to touch him.

"Dad. Christ. What happened?" She whispered, her voice cracking, certain she was about to be sick.

Harry reached out to her with his good arm, his hand shaking. "It's alright love. I'm fine. Sit down."

The kettle hissed into life and Monique turned from her post.

"Erica, I thought maybe tea but now I'm thinking something stronger." She didn't wait for a response and instead turned to Harry.

"How about some whisky? Or brandy?"

"No." Said Erica abruptly, still standing by her father. Only Monique could think of booze at a time like this. "He might need to go to hospital."

"I'm OK. I'm OK." Said Harry gently speaking over his daughter.

"What about your arm, your head? What happened?"

Harry took a breath and stared up at the ceiling. "When I came back today, I disturbed someone in the house." He looked his daughter in the eye and ran his tongue tentatively over his swollen lips, tears coursing down his face.

"I'll get the whisky." Said Monique and clipped purposefully out of the room.

Erica had seen battles going on inside Harry before, usually when on the subject of her mother when she was a teenager, but he had never lost to tears before. It was a disturbing and uncomfortable sight.

"We've got to call the police now." She said squatting down beside him. "Dad this is awful. We've got to call them now. I'll call Connor too, he'll know what to do. We can't just sit here and do nothing. Someone's really hurt you."

Harry was all the time shaking his head. She drew away and reached for the kitchen roll, ripping off a few sheets and passing them to him.

She looked momentarily towards the hall and then back to Harry. "Did they take anything? Oh my god dad. Oh my god. Look at you. What did they do? Did you see who it was?"

Harry was still shaking his head. He dabbed at his eyes gently, one puffy and maroon, and took a long sniff.

"No love. I'll call the police later, I will. Later." He repeated. "I just want to wait a while." Harry paused, gently tracing the seam of his shirt along his bruised arm with an index finger. "It brought up a few things for me. I just need to wait a while. I wanted to see you first."

"How could anyone want to hurt you?" Erica's voice was high, cracking. "This wasn't meant to happen."

Monique returned with three generous measures of whisky, placed the cut crystal glasses heavily on the table and went to the freezer for some ice.

Erica was muttering now. "I don't understand. Things have been getting better, there's been less... trouble."

"Here." Said Monique, handing the largest measure to Harry. He took a deep, lingering slug without hesitation.

Erica frowned at Monique. "Dad might need to go to hospital." She said again, directing her personal despair at the one person in the room she wished would vanish. Her stomach was marching around her abdomen. The thought of applying alcohol to it in its current state was repulsive to her.

"Did he kick you in the head?" Erica turned back to her father, her eyes meeting his with a new understanding, one that Monique was not yet party to. Her stomach lurched and in one movement she was bent over the sink throwing up in hot pulses, the best of Starbucks reduced to a slippery, acidic mush.

Monique was by her side at once turning on the taps and cooing, pulling Erica's hair from her face and then tearing off acres of kitchen roll to dab at her mouth. Harry got to his feet and moved to her other side, speaking quietly and gently in her ear, softly rubbing the top of her back.

"He didn't hurt my head love. It's fine. It barely hurts that much, it's mainly my arm. It didn't last long. I bruise easily. Really love. My head doesn't hurt at all. I bash it harder than this at work all the time." His words came out slowly, measured, loaded with comprehension for Erica's physical reaction. "I'm hard as nails. Really. Don't worry about it."

Erica put her head under the tap and rinsed her mouth. She turned to her father and they held each other for a minute.

"You're sure?" She said.

"I'm sure."

In a few minutes they collected themselves, Harry insisting that they move to the sitting room where Erica finally got to listen to Harry's account of events.

He made short work of his explanation – factually there was relatively little to tell. He explained that it was over quickly after the intruder had left him in the lounge. The man had spoken gruffly, according to Harry, as if trying to hide his natural diction through a deep and feeble mumble: "I haven't made too much of a mess." He had said and then departed via the dining room to empty the sideboard of its contents, deftly smashing the lock on the way.

Harry had remained hunched, dripping blood onto the hearth, listening to the tick tick ticking of the radiators until Monique had returned home only fifteen minutes later.

He was calm now, he explained, wounded and little shaken yes, but calm all the same.

Erica sat in silence at first, chewing at her nails, irritated by the lack of detail – no face to go on, only silverware and jewellery taken as far as they knew. She went over everything with Harry, picking apart the moments he had described to her, wanting more than he could give, stalling over what little had been said by the intruder.

"'I've come to take what's mine'?" She queried, sitting opposite Harry on the same footstool, as he leant back into the sofa. Monique was up and down, in and out of the room, wiping gently at Harry's drying blood on the dark stone hearth, then disappearing to find a more vigorous detergent. She had heard the story once before and had asked the same questions.

"That's what he said." Said Harry.

"We've really got to call the police dad. Like *now*."

Harry again stalled his daughter.

"Later love, really. Just give me a moment. We'll go down later, I promise." He sat back, catching Monique's eye as she returned, nodding to her to sit down. She perched on the end of the sofa, legs crossed.

"It's a bit strange to me though, my reaction to it all. He's no bigger than me, and certainly not much younger."

"How do you know?" Asked Monique, fiddling with a pair of yellow rubber gloves. "You said you didn't see his face."

"True. But I know. I know *him*." Harry announced, touching his nose gently, pressing for sensation.

Erica was momentarily stunned.

"Or at least I think I do." He went on. "But that's not the point. The point is that's not the reason I didn't retaliate. And I'm not too proud to admit when I'm wrong or have lost a battle." He aimed this last statement at Monique. "It just felt as if I reached inside myself for the response, for the enragement I would expect to feel under the circumstances, and there was nothing there. I would have hit him if I could. But I couldn't."

"You mean you felt like a victim?" Asked Monique. "That's a normal response I'm sure – helplessness."

"No. Not like a victim." Harry swigged the last of the whisky from his glass and cupped it in both hands. "It was more like the whole thing was a form of retribution. My body wasn't capable of any violent response. Nor should it have been necessarily."

I can't believe I'm hearing this. Erica's mouth was dry. He coat was hanging off her shoulders and she shuffled feebly to break free from it. It was her turn for exceptional and crushing discovery. Harry, her father, consumer of Oxfordshire's finest brews, now a victim of her own meddling.

For that moment she was glad of Monique's persistence to be part of the seeming unravelling that was taking place before her – it gave her time to put it all together.

"Do you mean that you did him wrong some time ago and he came for what was his? I assumed this was the same person that has been breaking into everyone's homes." Monique's face was screwed up, her expression bordering on horrified.

"No. I don't mean retribution for anything I did to *him*." Harry drew breath and placed the heavy glass on the floor in front of him. "I mean for the past. It's been hanging over me for years. Perhaps today was pay back. What I mean is, that you could argue that I got what was coming to me. Only I didn't realise it *would* come to me. I didn't expect it to. But it did. And in the grand scheme of things, I accept that."

Monique opened her mouth to speak, still frowning, but had run out of questions given the diminishing sense that Harry was making of his explanation of events. Erica could see from her peripheral vision that Monique was looking her way for support but chose to ignore her.

"I don't understand." Was all Erica could say. She wondered if Harry was holding back because of Monique's presence, adding to the already vexing impact of his uncharacteristic delivery. Harry wasn't a complicated beast but he sat before her now, digging around for different ways of saying she knew not what. He must be concussed. He'd hit his head harder than he thought he had. Her father spoke in simple terms, not in riddles; he didn't *allude* to anything and he certainly didn't use words like 'retribution'. And he had never drawn on the past in such a wistful manner, unless of course, in reference to Dorothy.

Monique, as if following Erica's thoughts, shuffled to the edge of her perch.

"Is this a family matter?" She ventured. "Because I can go."

Harry closed his eyes and shook his head. "No, you stay. I can't hide from things. It's best you know anyway." He forced a half smile and turned to Erica.

"Darling." He began, again not a word Harry normally used in addressing his daughter. He wriggled in his seat as if preparing for a speech but was stalled by the front door opening and footsteps in the hall. Erica saw Janice march past into the kitchen and then out again, evidently in haste to find someone. She spotted Erica sitting by the unlit fire and stopped in the doorway, her face flushed with recent tears. From her position Janice could see neither Harry nor Monique, her line of sight blocked by the open door.

Erica held up her hand to stop whatever was about to come from Janice's mouth. It was in vain.

"Keith had a vasectomy. Four years ago apparently. We've been trying for more children ever since the twins Erica. Every bloody month I'm watching my dates, timing it all, losing the plot with excitement if I'm late, and all this time he knew it would never happen. He bloody well *knew*. Can you believe that? He had keyhole surgery *behind* my back. Worst of all, he told Cleo, years ago when he did it. She's known all the time. He finally admitted it this morning when I told him I'd been to enquire about IVF and well – "

Monique coughed politely and Janice stopped. She stepped into the lounge and recoiled to see first Monique and then Harry on the sofa and the apparent damage to Harry's face.

Monique stood up. "I'll make some coffee."

"Jesus. Sit DOWN!" Said Erica, her words penetrating the room in a kind of yelp. "This is turning into a flipping farce."

Everyone was silenced. Janice gingerly stepped in and hovered on the other side of the fireplace. She blew loudly into a handkerchief and crouched to place her bag gently on the hearth, into the smeared blood that was only half wiped away. Monique noticing, raised her hand and went to speak, appeared to think better of it and withdrew, sliding down into the corner of the sofa.

"What happened to you dad?" Asked Janice quietly.

Harry repeated the events of the afternoon to Janice, patiently and slowly, and Janice asked many of the same questions that Monique and Erica had asked already.

"It's not a bad thing that you're here." Said Harry. "I was about to explain a few things to Erica, about what happened to your mother."

Janice, finally adjusted to the situation she had entered, slid down the wall and pulled her knees up to listen.

"Before I start, Janice I'd be grateful if you could let me speak to the end without interruption."

Without repetition, hesitation or deviation thought Erica and in the same instant, scolding herself.

Janice cocked an eyebrow but surrendered to Harry's request by saying nothing.

"You probably remember Erica, when your mother died, that she fell down the stairs shortly beforehand."

Erica nodded, her stomach weak and empty, heart racing through a pattern of random and uncomfortable palpitations.

"Well, she and I had just had a row, the reason being that I'd strayed." Harry paused, stroking his arm again. "I'd had an affair with someone. Ever so briefly I might add, but an affair nonetheless. She hated me, your mother, she was full of rage when I told her and rightly so, and I was begging her to keep it quiet so as not to upset you girls. Anyway, it was the end of a long day and she was just home from work – I hadn't really picked my moment very well – she had one shoe on and one shoe off and was trying to get away from me as quickly as possible. I remember it all like it was yesterday." His voice cracked and he coughed to bring himself back. "She made for the stairs and fell in her haste."

Janice shuffled, appearing to struggle with herself to remain silent. Erica stared at her father disbelievingly.

Harry paused again, fighting with tears a second time.

"You know the rest love, as we all do, and I stand by what the specialists said to this day and that is that the haemorrhage was waiting to happen." Harry's voice was climbing and he swallowed to bring it down. "But your sister..." He nodded to Janice, "Has always blamed me for what happened." Harry sniffed and dabbed at his nose again. "And that's the other bit that you didn't know about. And that's the bit that I think's all wrapped in today – my injuries. What you might call *karma* perhaps."

Janice's mobile sprang into life from within her handbag and she groped around ineptly to silence it.

Erica's mouth was dry. She was stunned by the overload of disturbing facts that had been thrust at her in less than half an hour. The unravelling felt monstrous – a cascade of unsavoury information provoking in that instant a numbness, a dejection at hearing about Harry's betrayal first hand and for being the last to know.

"Right." She said in a whisper, clueless as to what to say or how to react. They were all guilty in some way, Harry for his long-held secrets, Janice for her unrelenting torment of him over the years and Erica for the massive crime that now gnawed away at her and who's consequences were now reaching into unfathomable personal territories.

"I thought you might have…" She swallowed uncomfortably. "… had an affair." Erica turned to Janice. "But what does Ellen think?" She asked, her syllables sticking from the dryness in her mouth.

Janice and Harry looked at each other and said nothing. Finally Janice spoke, the silence she took to be Harry's approval that she rejoin the discussion.

"She sat on the fence for a while and hasn't really wanted to be drawn on it." Janice sighed. "Out of loyalty to me I suspect. She believed mum's condition was a time bomb. She researched it afterwards I understand – as did we *both*." She glared at Harry and then turned back to Erica, hands clasped around her shins, knees drawn up. "It was different for me, I'd done my time in on the wards and I never think these things are black and white. There's always a possibility that these conditions can be… kick started into action, if you like. Mum *could* have had…" Janice turned to Harry again, this time without malice, but with resignation in her voice. "… more time. Worse, that the last thing she comprehended was the fact of her husband's betrayal." She finished on a loud sigh, appearing to draw back to her own related discovery of the day.

"But it was still going to happen, right?" Asked Erica, the muscles in her chin twitching, turning to her father for reassurance, his rock-like status diminishing with every passing minute.

"Yes." Harry nodded.

"Yup." Janice agreed quietly.

Erica stood up, her legs feeble, head thumping.

"I can't stand this. This has to be the worst day of my life. Well, second worst…" She trailed off. "We're like some kind of bloody soap opera."

Without anyone noting it, Monique slid to the edge of the sofa and stood up too. When she addressed the room Janice and Erica seemed almost surprised by her presence.

"No one deserves what happened to you today Harry." She said. "No matter what is in the past. We all make mistakes don't we? But karma or fate or call it what you like, it doesn't wait ten years, it doesn't act in so precise a manner if it acts at all. There wouldn't be murderers roaming free if it did. We're all simply human and we're all fallible. You made a mistake but I don't think you're paying for it now."

Harry was shaking his head in penitent disagreement.

"This is my family we're talking about here Monique." Said Erica, worn out, facing Monique upright. "We can't just reduce it down to a bunch of clichés. We're worth more than that."

Monique continued, choosing to ignore Erica's rebuff. "Erica, you and I should get some dinner on." She thumbed like a hitchhiker to indicate that they vacate the room. "And you two have some talking to do."

Harry and Janice looked at the floor, silenced by Monique's assertiveness.

"When you've finished, we eat, then we call the police. They're bound to want to come here and check the place out so all the better they do it at night when there's fewer people to see. Janice, I'll get you a glass of wine. You look like you could do with one." Finally, she turned to Harry. "Harry, if you're so sure you know who he was, you need to let someone know. I'm guessing he's local and I'm guessing you know he's not going anywhere just now."

Harry nodded.

Erica bent down to kiss her father on the head as she made to leave the room.

"I'm sorry dad."

"Don't be sorry love. There's nothing for you to be sorry for. It's me."

Monique held out her hand, gesturing as if to lead a child to safety. Erica took it, finally caving in to Monique's relentless pursuit of being the comfort-giver.

Feeling pathetic, feverishly contemplating the skewed results of her actions she headed towards the door with her, stopping to make one final comment to Harry.

"He's not a big beer drinker this man, is he?" She asked.

Harry frowned and slowly shook his head.

"No."

She projected feebly in her mind other possible, similar consequences of her actions, but it became muddied with newly established facts about Harry.

"Oh, and there is one more thing you ought to know." Harry said with a returning strength to his voice. "The woman was a friend of Anita Singh's."

Erica's mind, hacked at, rearranged and stuffed together with new interconnections, took a second to realise who 'the woman' was that Harry was referring to.

"Anita Singh. Your boss."

"I know who my boss is." Whispered Erica flatly.

"Well, she knows about what happened."

Erica looked back at Harry who seemed entirely pathetic at that moment.

"Great."

TWENTY

Erica sat in her car outside the Old Rectory. She was parked in the driveway beside a 'Sold' sign that leant at forty-five degrees from a bed of daffodils. The gears were disengaged, the engine purred quietly and warm air poured over her feet and hands. She turned the volume up at the signature tune of the hourly news programme.

A car mechanic has been convicted today of eight burglaries and six assaults in the Brenly-on-Thames area. The court was told that Frank Arkwright, a fifty-eight-year-old resident of the town, broke into a number of his client's homes and in some cases assaulted them, over a period of ten months. He was eventually identified by his most recent victim.

Prosecutor Alex Cornweal described Arkwright as a loner that had abused the trust of neighbours and clients. Arkwright's ancestors had lived in Brenly-on-Thames for several hundred years. His grandfather squandered most of the family fortune but had arranged for what remained of his properties to be leased to the church upon his death. A loophole in the law had allowed the church to sell the property in the last century. Arkwright became obsessed with this and in his defence, claimed to be avenging his family's name by stealing from a number of the houses.

Detective Superintendent Mary Sandford said: "We're pleased with today's conviction. Arkwright showed a total disregard for those who had come to trust him over the years and had demonstrated an unhealthy obsession with the past." He will be sentenced at Oxford Crown Court next Tuesday.

Erica switched the radio off.

"I still can't believe it was Frank. He's been fixing our cars for as long as I can remember. You'd never have suspected him for a nutter."

Carmi, sitting beside her in the passenger seat, nodded. "You never do." She sipped through the plastic lid of a coffee cup and gingerly swivelled in her seat to face her friend. "So how is he then, your dad, how's he doing?"

"Not so bad. The sale seems to have gone through quickly enough." Erica leant behind to the back seat and rummaged in a worn plastic storage box. "I told you didn't I that he and Monique are going on a cruise in the summer with the equity? Well, some of it."

"Yes you did. Sounds like a plan."

Erica pulled a pair of secateurs from the box and swivelled round again. "Sounds like a plan indeed. I honestly thought she was after his money but she insists she's going to carry on teaching." She flicked the safety catch to snap the secateurs open and flicked it back again. "As long as he's happy."

Erica turned the engine off and pulled at the door handle. "I'm just going to cut some of these flowers." She sighed. "I should have really brought my camera. Or is that a bit naff?"

Carmi looked at her, a loose woollen hat sitting low above her eyebrows, and shrugged.

"You're the sentimental one honey, not me. And you're handling this all remarkably well. So, do whatever you have to do." She linked her hands around the paper cup and sucked noisily from it.

Erica made a quiet "Hmmm," and regretted asking what now seemed to be a stupid question.

Carmi went on. "But are you happy now Erica? Is all this stuff behind you?"

Erica said nothing and went to step out of the car. Carmi held her free arm gently to stop her.

"I'm serious. Is your appetite for trying to fix everything finally sated?"

"Carmi, please."

"You're lucky that none of that stuff had serious side effects. I mean it's one thing to be altering the temperament of the beer drinking faction of an entire county but quite another to prevent Oxford United losing every match in the first half of the season because they weren't in the mood for attack."

Erica smiled weakly. "I didn't forget about the brewery sponsorship. I just didn't think that any of them actually drank the stuff." She looked at Carmi quizzically. "God that can't be real can it? They didn't lose because of me did they?"

Carmi frowned, pushing her hat further down her brow. "Sometimes I don't know when you're being serious."

Erica reached out an index finger and poked Carmi playfully in the arm. "I said I've finished with it all. And you said you'd keep it a secret."

"I know and I will. But you were playing with fire last year Erica. Sometimes I think about it and I just …" Carmi waved her hand in the air to find the words and shook her head theatrically. "I dunno. Seriously. It's an understatement to say you were playing with fire. It was so much more than that. It was great big Krakatoas full of the stuff. I mean, look at it for what it was. Normally, *normally*, human nature would drive a person to fix something in a staged way – little by little – try this, then that, and if it doesn't work, try something else. But you went straight for the jugular. But not only that, I can't believe you thought you could actually… well, play God."

Erica cocked her head, irked by the rehashing of her actions but intent on keeping things light.

"And anyway, Krakatoa was pyroclastic flows and ash. Not *fire* as such."

"OK. You were playing with potentially cataclysmic pyroclastic flows! That better? You know what I mean. But seriously. I'm losing the thread of my own analogy – metaphor? Whatever." Carmi stopped and looked at her friend curiously. "Did you tell Harry what happened to you all those years ago?"

"No."

"Why not?"

"Same reason as always. There's no point. So I got mugged. So I got mugged three days after mum died. I couldn't tell him then because it was absolutely the wrong time. And there's no point telling him now. There's too much unravelling going on as it is. And anyway…" Erica shuffled uncomfortably. "It wasn't such a big deal. He just took my bag, pushed me over. After the event, when life got back to normal, well, OK last year… the whole thing just ignited the, well… the feminist in me."

"The *feminist*? The crackpot chemist more like."

"Carmi." Erica whined through her nose.

"You're clever Erica. But you should have used another outlet for whatever it is that's been driving you though. Like talked to someone. Like talked to me."

"Or just grow up you mean."

"Well, that too. I thought I had some of that under control, but evidently not."

"I'm not sure that I can." Erica had one foot on the gravel and was becoming uncomfortable in straining back to speak. "Can I go now?"

"Go on then. We've got to get changed presumably before we meet Duncan Spunken later."

"And Georgia. She's lovely. You'll really like her. She's down for the weekend."

Carmi tilted her head back and drained the last of the coffee from her cup.

"I feel like I'm coming along to baby-sit. I'm not sure why you want me there."

"It'll be fun. Duncan's got these free tickets for the comedy club. I don't see the harm. I kinda feel sorry for him because I think he wants Georgia to think he's got lots of friends. *And…* I can sort of understand that 'cos they did meet in a virtual world after all."

"I just can't believe you still wanna hang out with him."

Erica got out of the car, turned noisily on the gravel and promptly knelt back on to the driver's seat.

"I'm really sorry Carmi. About everything. You've been so understanding."

"I haven't really Erica. I don't truly understand. I admire you for what you tried to do but you were bloody stupid too."

Erica looked down and fiddled with the secateurs again.

"And no, I won't tell a soul. I can't. How can I? I'm complicit now." She continued. "But anyone would think that you were acting on some kind of personal revenge. You're just lucky that Connor never smelt a rat."

"I know. I thought that keeping him at arm's length would be tricky, but he's not exactly chomping at the bit to see me these days. Oh dear…"

Carmi looked at her friend expectantly and said nothing.

Erica pulled her head up and caught her stare.

"I just wanted to do my bit."

They looked at each other, Erica wavering uncomfortably on one knee, unwilling to take the subject further.

Carmi shook her head and waved dismissively at her. "Off you go then. Get picking."

Erica shuffled out of the car, relieved to be free of the conversation. She stood for a minute, feet planted on the ground, watching drifts of sunlight come and go through broken clouds that lit the stonework of the Old Rectory in brilliant pulses. The daffodils caught a tide of chilly spring air and Erica walked up to the broadest bed, and then through it, stepping around the stalks until she was in the centre. She looked back at Carmi and smiled: she was absorbed, deftly thumbing her phone.

The end of the greenhouse was just visible from where Erica was standing and she squinted to see what Harry had left behind: a stack of plastic seedling trays and a sturdy aged garden fork propped against the door to keep it closed. Erica squatted down and looked among the daffodils, more crowded than before, and, taken with a childish urge to find the perspective she craved in that instant, knelt and then pushed her body forwards, crushing a dozen stems underneath her, her eyes level with the lively yellows that invaded her line of sight. Long green leaves hung close to her face and she smiled, taking in the brisk perfume that pervaded ground level, focusing and unfocusing her eyes. She pressed her fingers through the smooth fabric of leaves, proud and fresh from the mulch of winter.

Printed in the United Kingdom by
Lightning Source UK Ltd., Milton Keynes
142265UK00001B/156/P